M000304591

Teach Me, Lord, to Dance
An Interview with Jesus

George W. Pettingell

Frankie Dove Publishing
Federal Way, Washington

Teach Me, Lord, to Dance

An Interview with Jesus

Dedication

Connie, you are dancing with the Lord now.
For the ten years that we were co-workers at KTBW-TV,
I saw you encourage so many people.
You made people feel welcome, you made them feel alive,
you gave them hope, and you made them special
because you reflected Jesus in your life.
Thank you for reading each chapter
as this interview with Jesus unfolded.
Thank you for your comments, your suggestions,
your encouragement, your cheerleading.
I look forward to seeing you again.

Connie Joan Waits
1957-2006

Acknowledgements

So many people contributed to this interview with suggestions, encouragement, and prayer. I wish I could name you all. The Lord knows who you are. You are special in His sight.

In particular I would like to give thanks to…

- Bette Filley, publishing consultant and owner of Dunamis Publishing in Issaquah, Washington, for your valuable insights into the world of publishing.
- Candace Gurney of Issaquah, Washington, because your special walk with the Lord confirmed many of the incidents in this interview with Jesus.
- Dr. Paul Wright, President of Jerusalem University College, who didn't know you were putting the finishing touches on this book as you led us through the Promised Land.
- Dr. Ben Cross, Senior Pastor of Grace Community Church in Auburn, Washington, for your suggestions that made the interview come alive with truth and faith.
- Bev Fowler, Editor, Consultant, and Founder/Leader of B Write Writing Workshops in Issaquah, Washington, for encouraging me to go beyond my comfort level.

Most of all, thanks to my wife, Karen, for your deep and abiding faith in our Lord Jesus Christ, your insight into Scripture, your gift of spiritual discernment, your daily encouragement, and your profound commitment to me for 42 wonderful years.

I must hasten to add that I am responsible for whatever mistakes there are in this interview. The truths revealed in these pages are to the glory of our Lord and Savior, Jesus Christ.

Preface

Teach Me, Lord, to Dance: An Interview with Jesus is based on the Bible. I have woven Scripture throughout the questions and responses, most often in paraphrase form and without Scriptural references. For those who desire chapter and verse notations, the last chapter, "Now What?" lists suggested references pertinent to each of the chapters.

At the same time, some of the statements and situations in the Interview are conjecture, assuming what Jesus might have said or done where the Gospels are silent. Yet even here I have attempted to be true to the spirit of Scripture and the nature of Jesus.

My hope is that the interviewer's questions might reflect your questions, and that the answers might speak to your situation, whatever it may be.

George W. Pettingell
December, 2006

Introduction

I have to say I'm intimidated by you.

There's no need to be intimidated. Just relax and be yourself.

In that case, let me get right to the point. Most people have no idea who you are or who you were. "Jesus Christ" is a swear word. That's all. Just a swear word. They could care less about you.

Nothing has changed, has it? When I lived on earth 2,000 years ago, most people didn't care about me, either. Some thought I was entertaining. They liked my stories and my miracles. Others thought I was too outspoken, that this peasant from the countryside had no right to challenge the "big boys." Still others thought I was a religious "nut" making a lot of noise and attracting a lot of attention only to be forgotten when my fifteen minutes were up. Only a few truly believed in me.

Yet you're here and they're the ones who are forgotten.

I'm still alive. They murdered me, but I came back to life, just as I said I would.

Why did you consent to this interview?

I want those who don't know me, who don't believe in me, to know that I am more than just a swear word or something to joke about or dismiss as fantasy or myth. I was more than just a "good" man, or a healer, or a teacher.

I want you to believe that I am the eternal, awesome, holy God of the entire universe. When you do believe, I will radically change your life. I will clean out those dark corners, give you new meaning and purpose, and make life worth living today and forever.

At the same time, I want those who do know me and believe in me to be encouraged and motivated, to know how urgent the times are.

I'm coming soon, and I want you to be ready.

Talking Points

You were a radical, weren't you?

You were a radical, weren't you?

Let me tell you about myself, then you tell me whether I was a radical or not.

People in my hometown tried to throw me off a cliff and kill me. They hated me. I looked the power elite in the eye and called them hypocrites.

I broke all the social taboos. I spent most of my time with outcasts, the people society threw onto the garbage dump of life, like the poor and the sick and the mentally deranged and prostitutes and tax collectors and those who just didn't amount to much in the eyes of the elite. Yet I ate dinner with the rich and met clandestinely at night with political leaders who sought my advice.

I was homeless. I didn't own anything and slept in the open except when people invited me to stay in their homes. My closest followers included fishermen and intellectuals and terrorists and tax collectors and even women. Huge crowds gathered around me everywhere I went, people who were curious, who were doubtful, who wanted a good show. Then there were those who honestly wanted to learn from me and feel my touch on their lives.

Political leaders didn't know if I was against the Roman occupation or a sympathizer with Rome. It infuriated them when I didn't take sides.

I knew when people were phony and when they were real. I could look into someone's soul and understand where they were coming from or what their hang-ups were or if they had problems or hurts. I listened and cried and laughed and healed and cast out demons and even raised people from the dead.

Some people called me God.

I called myself God.

You admitted to that at the very beginning of our interview, "I am the eternal, awesome, holy God of the entire universe."

What do you think? Was I a radical?

Maybe radical isn't strong enough. A revolutionary? A crazy? A religious nut? An entertainer? A con man?

Even you don't know what to think about me, do you? Most people were like you. They couldn't figure me out. Here was this "country boy" who was attracting tremendous crowds. I had an authority that even these so-called leaders didn't have. I wasn't afraid or intimidated. I didn't cower before them.

People who had everything—power, prestige, money—hated me. Those who didn't have anything loved me.

You didn't take the easy way out, did you? You continually got in people's faces.

I didn't pull any punches. I told it the way it was. And I did what needed to be done. For example, I spent time with lepers. They had these ugly sores all over their bodies and smelled awful. Lepers were the ultimate outcasts. They were not even supposed to get close to "normal" people. If they got within shouting distance, they were to yell out a warning first that they were unclean. But what did I do? I walked right up to them and reached out and touched them. You weren't supposed to do that. It was just not done. But I did it. And they walked away healed. I didn't do this just once, but all the time.

So people believed in you because you were a miracle worker? A healer? A phony?

I thought you said you were intimidated by me.

Yeah, well...

Let me tell you something. I really did heal people—a woman bent over for 18 years, a man born blind, people who were deaf, crippled, maimed, mentally ill. I did it in the open, for all to see. The authorities tried to prove it false, saying that these people really weren't healed, that I was a phony. But they couldn't refute what happened. The blind man told it best, "I know only one thing. I was blind, but now I see!"

I did what I did, and said what I said, because I loved people. My love was not, and is not, a mealy-mouthed love, or a syrupy love, or a "you're ok-I'm ok" love. It's a love that encompasses everyone and accepts everyone. It's a love of forgiveness, of understanding, a love that's above race and nationality and "religion," a love of justice and mercy and peace. My love is a divine, holy love—a love that was sorely lacking in that society and in your society today.

15

I understood, I cared, I listened. I taught what people had heard all their lives, but in a way that was different, that made sense. I put my words into action. I loved people with a genuine, no-strings-attached love.

How can you talk about love when you hated some groups of people so much? That hypocrisy thing, for example. Why did you call the religious leaders hypocrites?

Hate isn't part of my agenda. I didn't hate them. I loved them, too. But I don't like hypocrisy, phoniness, bluster, make believe. They should have known better. They were the religious leaders of their day. They were supposed to set the moral and religious example. Some example! They lived for the adoration people gave them, walking around in their expensive clothes, greeted by everyone in the market place, sitting in the front seats at meetings and in the best seats at banquets, praying long prayers to show how religious they were. Yet they cheated widows out of their homes.

I don't like show-offs, when people think they are better than others. I don't like it when people flaunt their riches and their trophies, or brag about how good they are or how high their position is in the church or in government or in business.

I want people to be servants, not masters, to have compassion, to walk in the shoes of others, to feel how they feel.

I abhor those who are "religious" but don't live the precepts of their religion. I called those people "whitewashed tombs, which on the outside look beautiful, but inside are full of bones and filth."

The religious leaders taunted you, didn't they?

They laughed at me, called me names, tried to make me look bad in front of the crowds. They were always puffing themselves up, trying to make themselves look good in the eyes of the people. It didn't work with me. I could see right through them. They were always looking for opportunities to make me look bad, to discredit what I was saying or doing. But I looked them in the eye and told them, "I see what's in your heart, and I don't like what I see. What you think is important is worthless as far as I'm concerned."

They called John a fool because he was a "wild man," a loner, living in the desert, dressed in animal skins, eating locusts and honey, standing in the Jordan River yelling that people had to get right with God, that the Messiah was coming. They honestly thought John was possessed by demons.

Then I came along, just the opposite. They said I was a party-goer, a do-gooder, a friend of those who were the outcasts of society. And they said I, too, was possessed by demons. The leaders tried to figure me out. Zealots thought I was the political messiah they had long waited for. Others were simply curious, attracted to my miracles, my teaching. Still others thought I was a threat to society and peace.

Then why did you associate with these "hypocrites"? Why did you eat and drink at their homes?

I told you who they were—self-righteous, self-important whitewashed tombs. People who couldn't stand me, but who wanted my popularity to rub off on them. Religious fundamentalists who didn't tolerate anybody who believed differently than they did. Tax collectors who sold out to the Romans and became filthy rich at the expense of their own Jewish brothers. And lawyers and physicians and politicians and bankers and Doctor this and Doctor that.

They did lots of posing, lots of posturing. But in truth they were hurting. They wanted what I offered, but couldn't afford to say so in front of their cronies. I wasn't the phony. They were.

You didn't answer the question. Why did you associate with these kinds of people?

It goes back to love. Even though they were hypocrites, which I detest, I loved them. Sounds contradictory, doesn't it? But it's not. They were lost. Sinners in need of forgiveness and redemption. They said the right things. They just didn't do it themselves. My Father sent me to these people. They didn't know what they were doing, like sheep without a shepherd. I didn't come to minister to those who were well, but to those who were lost and sick.

But they didn't believe in you, did they?

Unfortunately, most of them didn't believe in me. ome did. Nicodemus and Joseph, for example. Nicodemus was a member of the highest religious body in the nation, and Joseph was very rich and prominent in the nation's politics.

Matthew and Zaccheus also believed. They were tax collectors, hated by the people and tolerated by the Roman authorities. Both of them gave up a lot—money, prestige, great retirement benefits—when they left their plush jobs to follow me. They suffered devastating ridicule from the Romans for becoming "religious fanatics."

That last time you went to Jerusalem, you went into the temple and turned over the tables of the money changers and the benches of those who were selling doves and lambs and other animals slated to be sacrificed. Why?

That was my Father's house. It was a place of worship, not a place of selling and extorting and confusion. The Scriptures say, "My house shall be called a place of prayer for all nations, but you have made it a place where robbers hide." Robbers were selling doves and lambs for exorbitant rates of money. They greatly inflated prices for the animals used in worship. I was angry. There's no place in my Father's house for that kind of thing. So, yes, I literally threw over the tables of the money changers and extortionists. I chased them out.

You challenged the religious leaders again the next day, didn't you?

I was teaching when a small group of religious leaders pushed a young, scared woman through the crowd and threw her on the ground in front of me. Her dress was torn and dirty, her face stained with tears. She was barefoot, hair disheveled.

"Teacher," they said, voices dripping with sarcasm, "we caught this woman in the very act of adultery. According to our Law, we are supposed to stone her to death. What do you think?"

They thought they were being clever, setting a trap that I couldn't get out of. If I said, "Let her go," I would be showing disrespect for the religious law. But if I agreed to her execution by stoning, I would be defying Roman law. Either way, I would jeopardize the very things I was teaching to the crowds—love and mercy.

The whole thing sickened me. They didn't care about this girl. She was a pawn in their morally corrupt hands. She was embarrassed, disgraced, publicly ridiculed. She knew nothing about the trap and, although she wasn't innocent, she was already sentenced to die in the minds of her accusers.

The accusers? They were holding big, sharp, jagged rocks, shifting them from hand to hand. Their eyes were full of hatred—cold, glassy, dilated. They could hardly wait to begin the massacre. The crowd was hushed, wondering what was going to happen, some of them hoping for blood. The girl's family was there, watching, weeping, horrified. Her husband was in the crowd, shamed and fearful.

I didn't say anything. I knelt and began to write in the dirt with my finger, at the same time listening to their hearts, giving these self-righteous judges time to think about what they were doing. My silence infuriated them. They thought I was ignoring them. They kept pushing for an answer. Finally, without looking up I said, "Okay, throw your stones. Whichever of you has never sinned, you throw the first stone."

Silence.

Still looking down, I wrote in the dirt again.

Silence.

Then one by one, the accusers dropped their rocks and left. These self-appointed judges, who were willing to see a young woman die because they wanted to discredit me and make themselves look good, left in disgrace.

The woman and I were left, the crowd waiting breathlessly to see how this would play out. I reached out and took the woman's hand. She was trembling.

"Look around you," I said. "Where did your accusers go? Has no one condemned you?"

"No one, Sir," she stammered.

"Look at me. Look into my eyes. I don't condemn you either. Go and don't do this again."

You weren't meek and mild, were you?

No. Not in today's meaning of the word—weak, puny, mousey, wimp, wuss. A meek person in today's vernacular is someone you can walk over, someone you can grind into the dirt with the heal of your shoe.

But I was meek and mild back then.

Give me a break. That's double talk.

Do you know what "meek" meant in those days?

I guess I don't. You better tell me.

It meant "power under control." Like a stallion that's been controlled. Not weak, but restrained, intense, spirited, ready to break free at any moment, to run, to feel the wind.

And that was you? Like a stallion? "Power under control?"

Under my Father's control, because I did only what He wanted me to do. I was the power of all heaven under control, serving the will of my Father and the needs of people. Under control—I loved people, I was patient, I was forgiving, but eager to run the race, to do what I was sent to do, to tell the truth, and to point out those things that were wrong.

You challenged your own nation's leaders. Did you ever challenge the Roman occupation? Did you get caught up in the radicalism, the terrorism, of your time, with the Zealots who tried to overthrow the Roman government?

I knew about it, of course. Nazareth, where I grew up, was just five miles from Sepphoris, the Roman capital of northern Israel. It was a magnificent city, the cultural and administrative center of our region. When I was in my teens, Joseph and I supplemented our carpentry business by working for the

21

Romans there. We helped build houses and public buildings, but our specialty was making furniture and doors and windows. Back in those days it was an art to build doors and windows that really worked.

That's interesting, but…

There were many people who hoped I would lead an insurrection against the Romans and end the occupation. They were deeply disappointed when I did nothing. I wasn't a Zealot. I didn't advocate open rebellion against Rome. But then I wasn't concerned about political things. I didn't come to overthrow the Romans. I came to overthrow the power of Satan over people's hearts and minds. I came to proclaim a radical love, rather than a radical political agenda. My Kingdom is about personal justice and mercy and love, those things that eternally change a man's soul, not just temporary fixes.

So you didn't say anything about the occupation? Wasn't one of your closest followers a Zealot?

Actually, two of my followers were Zealots—Simon and Judas. Zealots hated the Romans. Every chance they got, they tried to subvert the Roman occupation. They were the terrorists of their day. There was a Roman garrison at Sepphoris. Zealots ambushed and killed Roman sentries, broke into military stores, burned down their armories, stole horses, sabotaged roads and water supplies.

Weren't Judas and Simon involved in this kind of thing?

Yes, before they began following me. Even when they joined up with me they continued to hate the Romans. But as time went on, and Judas and Simon saw what I was all about, they began to change. The turning point came when the Roman centurion came to me asking if I would heal his servant. What courage he had, and faith. It had a profound effect on all my followers.

Okay, so what ultimately happened to the Zealot movement?

When the Romans caught Zealots, they crucified them. Sometimes they were lined up and down the main highways. Hundreds of them. Nailed to crosses, left to die a slow, tortuous death, for the birds to finish off. That was the Roman way of death, very cruel. Even though Joseph and I stayed out of politics, the Romans forced us to make crosses, to smooth out the wood and put the notches in the uprights for the cross bars.

You may have made your own cross?

Crosses were used again and again since wood was relatively scarce. Eventually they became soaked with blood.

So you were involved with the Romans in a sense. Zealots were among your followers. You enjoyed parties. You ate with the religious intelligentsia of the day. You made friends of the poor and the sick and the outcasts. You were very much a part of your world.

Let me put it this way. I embraced the world, I was involved in the world. But I didn't buy into it. I was concerned about man's relationship to God. That's where the real difference was and is. Was I a radical? Yes, indeed! Do you think that I came to bring peace to earth? To pat people on the head and say how nice it is to be nice? No! I came to set the earth on fire. I came to make people choose sides.

Why did you heal?

Okay, let's talk about this healing thing. When you healed people, what was it like? I mean, some people you touched and some people you just said a word to but didn't touch. Other people you put something on them, like spitting on some dirt then putting it on their eyes. Other times you reached out your hand and lifted them up, and they were healed. Still other times you healed people at a distance. You weren't even present when they were healed.

It doesn't matter how I did it. The point is that I did it. Many of those I healed had been afflicted by their sickness or infirmity for a long time, sometimes from birth. People who knew the person had seen the problem over the years, the physical deterioration. The person wasn't acting, the disease wasn't just in its first stages. One man had been blind from birth, another man crippled from birth, a woman had had an issue of blood for 12 years.

With the woman who had the bleeding problem, you felt power go out from you, and you said "who touched my clothes?" She didn't touch you, just your clothes. But you felt it. Did you feel some kind of energy transfer from you to her?

Yes, sometimes like a sudden burst and other times like wave after wave. I always knew I'd healed someone because the power would go out of me and into them, touch them and heal them and make them well. It was like my life force was drawn to them like a magnet. Yet I never felt drained. The energy was always there, for the next person and the next and the next.

Why did you heal people? I mean, it seems like that's all you did at the very beginning before you did much teaching. You healed people, and you never seemed to turn anyone away. Did you ever turn anyone away? What about Lazarus? His sisters, Mary and Martha, asked you to come, but you didn't. So in a sense you said, "No I won't heal you." But why all the healing? What was the purpose in that?

Whoa! One question at a time! First—I had, and I always will have, a deep, unceasing compassion for those afflicted with disease and illness. I love all people so much. I don't like to see people hurt and in pain and suffering. Unfortunately, when sin entered into the world through Adam, your bodies and minds became susceptible to illness and disease. This is one of the curses of sin. But, you see, I feel your pain so intensely that I want to help you bear that pain. I want to see you healed and be made well, if you will let me and if it is in your best interest.

Secondly—I want you to know this—I never healed or performed miracles to display my power or to create a sensation.

I never paraded my power or performed a miracle to satisfy someone's unbelief. I always used my power to aid and relieve those who were in need. That applies to today, as well. If you want the "wow" factor, don't look to me. I absolutely will not give in to it. I don't need it. And neither do you. That's not the way I do things.

Did I ever say no to someone who asked for healing? Yes, though not in so many words. Even today I sometimes say no, while sometimes I heal immediately. And other times I heal layer by layer, so to you it seems to take a long time. But to answer your question, yes, sometimes I say no.

What? I'm shocked! I thought you always healed. You never turned people away.

You mentioned Lazarus. When Mary and Martha sent word to me to come immediately because he was sick, I continued doing what I was doing for two days, then it took me two more days to walk to his town of Bethany. Now, I could have healed him, even from a distance. I didn't have to be there to do it. But I didn't, and by the time I got to Bethany four days later, he was dead and in the grave.

So, in a sense, you said no to Mary and Martha's request for you to heal Lazarus of his sickness?

That's right. But what did I do when I got to Bethany? I raised Lazarus from the dead. He had been dead for four days, and his body was already decaying. It really smelled! If I had healed Lazarus when his sisters wanted me to, it would have been a wonderful miracle. But raising him from the dead was the turning point of my ministry. It allowed me to proclaim to Martha who I was and who I am—the Resurrection and the Life. Those who believe in me will live even if they die.

27

And it allowed Martha to admit publicly, "Lord, I believe. You are the Messiah, the Christ, the Son of God. You are the one we hoped would come into the world."

The raising of Lazarus led to my crucifixion which led to my resurrection which leads to life everlasting for those who believed in me then and who believe in me now.

So...today as then, I don't always heal when you want me to heal. I know the whole picture. You don't.

What about the daughter of the rabbi? He asked you to come and heal his daughter because she was about to die. But you took time with that woman with the issue of blood. You healed her, but by the time you got to the rabbi's house, his daughter was dead.

Same answer. I raised her to life when I got there. And the Father received the greater glory because of it.

Another situation where you didn't heal someone was the man lame from birth.

Everyday his friends would carry him to the door of the temple to ask for alms from those going into the temple. This had been going on every day for 40 years. I walked past him many times. I could have healed him, but I didn't. I left that to Peter and John after my ascension to heaven. When they healed him, the man was able to walk on his own for the first time in his life. He was actually leaping and praising God as he went into the temple with Peter and John. All the people there saw it, and they were filled with astonishment and amazement about what had happened. God was glorified so much more by this healing than if I had done it during my lifetime.

So, when you didn't heal people, when you said "no," the outcome was greater than if you had said "yes"? And

that holds true for today, as well, when you say "no" when people pray for healing?

That's right. You see, healing is from me. You don't know all the details or all the reasons why or why not I might heal someone. Everyone's healing journey is different, because they are different, with different life styles and needs and circumstances. It is for me to decide. I will tell you this—what I do is always the best for those involved. It might not seem like it at the time, but it is always for their best. No, I didn't heal the illness that led to Lazarus' death, and I didn't get to the bedside of the little girl in time, and I didn't heal the crippled man at the Beautiful Gate. But they were all healed in a way that glorified the Father even more.

The bottom line is this, healing is not about you. It's about me.

Is sickness the result of a person's sin?

No. You are human. Since the fall of mankind, you live in a mortal, imperfect body that is subject to sickness and disease. Sometimes you bring sickness on yourself, because of what you eat or don't eat or picking up germs from others who have a disease or sickness. Sometimes God allows you to become ill as a means of teaching you about His goodness and His glory.

Can a person's lack of faith prevent their healing?

Yes. Faith is the key to healing. Look in the Scriptures at all the people I healed (and there were many, many more I healed who are not recorded in Scripture). They were all healed either by their faith or by the faith of a mother or father or the faith of someone associated with them. That's the key—faith. That's another reason why I didn't heal at times. People didn't believe I could do it, so I didn't. There were even places—entire towns—

where I was prevented from healing because the people there had no faith in me.

If you don't want to be healed, I won't heal you. As long as someone has faith, there's a possibility of healing. But if there is no faith, I won't heal that person. I'm not going to circumvent their will.

When I heal, it might not be for you, the one who needs to be healed. Yes, you might be the object of the healing, but the blessing of that healing might be for someone else. For example, when I raised Lazarus from the dead, it wasn't for Lazarus. He didn't want to come back! He was in a far better place. His healing, his raising from the dead, was for Mary and Martha. It was for the people who were witnessing it. It was for the religious leaders who heard about it. It was what led to my own death and resurrection. It wasn't for Lazarus.

Did you enjoy healing people?

Yes, very much. You might think that after a while, healing would have become automatic, or I might have said, "Oh, no, here comes another one to be healed," or with all the crowds pushing in on me it might have become an assembly line. But, no, it never was. Each one was exciting to me, to see my people become whole again and to see their reactions. It greatly saddened me, however, when some I had healed weren't thankful. They just took it for granted. When you are healed, the Father wants you to thank Him and give Him the glory.

What did you teach?

You did more than heal, didn't you? You taught, you preached. Why?

God sent me to proclaim good news to those who think they have everything but really don't have anything. He sent me to people who live broken lives, to those who are blind and deaf, who are tied and bound with chains of guilt and misery. God sent me to bring light to those who live in darkness.

You taught and preached wherever you could, didn't you?

I taught wherever people found me. I didn't have to seek them out. They sought me out. I preached in private homes and in public meeting places, in temples and in hovels, from a boat anchored off shore, in graveyards, by a well, on mountain sides, and while walking on dirt roads from town to town. I wanted to reach out to people wherever they were.

My message was that God is here, right now. He is not distant, but here, right where you are. He wants to give you life—abundant life. He wants to change your life and make you new. It's good news. A simple message, but straight to the point.

You were different from other teachers, weren't you? You spoke with authority, with power...

What I said wasn't new. Others before me had taught the same thing. But I knew what I was talking about. I had an intense desire to give people hope and encouragement. I didn't give multiple choices or fill in the blanks. I gave answers people could trust and believe in.

You didn't merely quote the opinions of others?

I just answered that question. But let me try again. I wanted the things of God to be understandable to my listeners. The truths of God aren't hidden, they're not "coded," they're not just for the "enlightened." I wanted to tell everyday people about God, who He is, how to find Him, how to know His awesome love. I wanted to motivate people, get them thinking.

And the people received it enthusiastically?

At first they did. Until I started saying things that were personal and hit home. I called people to task about how they lived their lives and their relationships with others. I pointed out where they had to change. People didn't like hearing that.

What specifically did you teach?

First of all you must love God with all of your heart, all of your soul, and all of your strength.

What does this mean?

It means that you are to love God first, before anyone else, and you are to love Him with all that you have. All of your emotions, all of your intellect, all of your very being.

And how do we do that?

By obeying Him. Giving Him first place in everything. Don't seek riches or success or the accolades of people. Do what He wants you to do. Realize that your very life depends on Him.

You get passionate about that, don't you?

Of course, I do. Your life, your very existence, comes from God. You need to do what He wants you to do.

What else did you teach?

That you are to love your neighbor as yourself.

What do you mean by that? Who is your neighbor?

That's an old question, but just as applicable today as ever. Your neighbor is anyone you come into contact with. The family who lives next to you and the single mom on the floor above and the eccentric old man on the floor below. The people you work with and do business with, those you socialize with and spend your time with, people you meet on the street or in the store or share the freeway with. Even people you don't particularly care about.

And to love your neighbor means...

Allow them to be themselves. Protect their dignity. Help them if they are hurting. Smile, be friendly, listen, encourage. Share with them if they are in need. Be a peacemaker. Treat people equitably and fairly. Try to understand where they are coming from and how you fit into that picture.

Be faithful in your relationships. Keep your promises.

Be an example to others. Cheer people up, give them hope, encourage them. Help them.

Don't take advantage of others. Don't make fun of others. Don't condemn or judge. Don't get even or seek revenge. Treat

33

other people as you would want them to treat you. Love your enemies. Be good to everyone who hates you. Pray for everyone who is cruel to you. If someone slaps you on one cheek, don't stop him from slapping you on the other cheek. If someone wants to take your coat, give him your shirt, too. Don't ask people to return what they have taken from you—

Now wait a minute. This is not realistic. You can't do that kind of stuff in the real world.

You asked. I answered.

Okay. I stand corrected. But you can't really do that stuff.

Sure you can. It's what I want you to do. The kind of attitude I want you to have.

Well…we'll leave that one alone for now. The next question is "why?" Why love God the way you say we should? Why love our neighbor?

You are to love God because He wants you to. Period.

That's it? Because He wants me to?

That's right. Because God wants you to. Now let me say this—God promises that if you love Him and put Him first in your life, He will take care of you. He will provide your food, your clothing, your physical needs, your emotional needs. Not that He will make you rich—He can if He wants to—but He will provide your needs and take care of you.

Let me emphasize this—You are not to love God because you expect His provisions in return. No. You love Him because He wants you to and because you just plain want to.

Why love your neighbor? Because God commands you to. He wants you to live at peace with everyone. He wants you to share His love. That's His way.

You said we should love our neighbor as we love ourselves. That means we are to love ourselves?

Yes. But it doesn't mean to puff yourself up, to be prideful, to think of yourself more highly than you should. To love yourself means to understand that you are special, that God made you and what He makes is good.

Loving yourself means that you forgive yourself. That you don't beat yourself over past mistakes. You don't go around having pity parties. The truth is, you really can't love others if you don't love yourself. I want you to forgive yourself and love yourself so that God's love and forgiveness can flow through you.

You got in trouble for teaching this stuff, didn't you? You upset people and got them angry with you?

Amazingly, yes. Those in power didn't like the authority I spoke with. They didn't like my talking about "hypocrites" and about pride. They felt that I was continually upstaging them.

I got in trouble. And it cost me my life.

Your mother was a virgin?

Let's go back to the beginning. You were born out of wedlock, weren't you?

No. I was conceived out of wedlock, but Mary and Joseph were married by the time I was born.

So you were illegitimate?

I wouldn't call it that. Mary was pregnant and not married, that's true.

Let me tell you the story. Mary was a teenage girl engaged to Joseph, who was in his 20s. But before they were married, Mary found out that she was pregnant. She didn't understand it, because she had never had sex with Joseph or with any other man. Joseph didn't believe her, and he was extremely upset that Mary would do this to him.

But Joseph was a good man and didn't want to shame Mary, so he decided to discreetly cancel the wedding. While he was thinking about it, Joseph had a dream in which an angel said to him, "Joseph, Mary is telling you the truth. She has not had sex with anyone. You've got to believe that. God's Spirit has come upon her and supernaturally caused her to become pregnant. God wants you to marry her but to abstain from sex until after the baby is born. When the baby is born, you are to name him Jesus."

That very same angel had appeared to Mary about a month before. He had told Mary that she would have a baby and would call him Jesus, because he would save his people from their sins. She was confused, to say the least, and argued with the angel, "How can this happen? I am a virgin." The angel told her that God's Spirit would come over her and impregnate her. She would be the baby's human mother, but God, Himself, would be the baby's father.

What was Mary's reaction?

She was scared. She didn't know how to handle all this. Imagine! She was an average teenage girl, interested in average teenage girl activities, when an angel appeared to her, telling her that she was to have a baby even though she was a virgin, and her son was to be the Savior of the world. Wow! What would she tell Joseph? What would she tell her parents? How would her relatives and friends and everyone in her small town react when they found out?

They wouldn't believe her. I wouldn't have. It's too preposterous. Sure, they would soon know that she was pregnant, and she would instantly become an outcast. They would probably stone her to death.

Mary didn't think of the consequences. She was too overwhelmed to think. With tears in her eyes, Mary said to the angel simply and meekly, "I am God's servant. May it happen as you have said."

The only person Mary could really confide in was her older cousin, Elizabeth. Elizabeth was extremely happy for Mary and reassured her, "Mary, you are most blessed, more than any other woman! You are blessed because you believed what God's angel said. And you are blessed because your son will be God, Himself, appearing in human form to save mankind from their sins."

Did anyone else believe?

Joseph believed when he and Mary compared stories. They both were visited by the same angel at different times who told them what to name me. The shepherds in the fields near Bethlehem believed when they saw me lying in that manger after the heavens opened up with angels singing about my birth. The wise men believed when they spent months following signs in the heavens that pointed to a king being born in Israel.

But no one else believed it. My own half brothers and half sisters didn't believe it. These were children born later to Mary and Joseph. Nobody in my hometown of Nazareth believed it. They thought I was the illegitimate son of Mary and Joseph.

I'm having trouble believing it. You were born through a woman supernaturally impregnated by God's Spirit?

That's right.

God was your Father?

That's right.

Okay…if you say so.

I do say so. That's the way it was.

We've got to get back to this. But let's go on. As a baby, did you realize that you were God? I mean, babies can't think, they don't understand language. They just lie there and do baby things. They have to grow into thinking beings.

Yes, even then I knew I was God. I knew who I was. Mary realized as only a mother could that I knew. She told me years later that when she and Joseph brought me to the temple in Jerusalem when I was eight days old to be purified and circumcised, she looked into my eyes. I returned her gaze with an intelligence that startled her. I understood the importance of my first entry into Jerusalem and that I would come here again, several times, until I had finished the work I had come for.

And yet you were a baby, just eight days old!

I was a baby, and I behaved like a baby. Mary breast fed me and changed my diapers. I cried when I was hungry or messy or tired. I was extremely trusting, and smiled easily. I thrived on love and radiated love. Even as a baby, I could hardly wait to go about my Father's business. I knew why I was here. But I had to wait for the right time to start doing what the Father had sent me to do.

In a sense, I was born an adult. My body just had to grow bigger until it caught up with my intelligence and my self-knowledge.

You have quite an imagination. Okay, continuing on. You were a refugee in your early years, weren't you?

Yes. Mary and Joseph and I had to flee Bethlehem because King Herod wanted to kill me. He was a jealous man, violent, insatiable. He had murdered most of his own family because he couldn't stand the thought of anyone taking his place as the so-called "King of the Jews." He decreed that thousands of citizens be killed on the day of his own death to ensure that there would be mourning during his funeral.

When Herod was told by the Wise Men—the astrologers from Persia who followed my star in the night skies—that another King of the Jews was born in Bethlehem, he sent soldiers to murder all male babies two years or younger in and around Bethlehem hoping that one of them would be me. Many babies died during this "slaughter of the innocents," but an angel once again appeared to Joseph telling him to take us immediately to Egypt. So we became refugees in Egypt until Herod died three years later, and it was safe to go back home.

How did the three of you exist? You had nothing.

We were strangers, foreigners. Joseph couldn't find permanent work, so we lived with other Jewish families, moving from family to family. Joseph sold the frankincense and myrrh the wise men had given me a little at a time so the authorities wouldn't get suspicious. Finally the gold ran out, as well.

When we came back to Israel we moved in with relatives in Nazareth.

Your first years of life weren't very auspicious, were they? I mean, you were born in a stable, surrounded by smelly farm animals. You fled to another country where you weren't accepted. When you came back you moved in with relatives. It's not a great way to grow up.

You know, it was my Father's plan. I came into the world to identify with all people, poor and rich, homeless and transient, the weak and the powerful. My message and my life were for everyone.

What were you like as a child?

As a toddler I was always on the move, first when I learned to crawl, then as I began to walk. I was fast. I wanted to explore everything. Mary had trouble keeping up with me. I played with pieces of wood and little toys that Joseph carved for me. I enjoyed life. I laughed easily, played with the neighbor children

41

my age. When I skinned my knees, I would run crying to Mary. She would hold me close, sing to me, and tell me how special I was. Sometimes she was exasperated. How could she handle someone who would act like a child one moment and like an adult the next?

I had picked up some Egyptian as a baby, and I was already reading in Aramaic and Hebrew by the time I was 18 months old. I was always jabbering in a mixture of those languages. I'm sure Mary and Joseph got tired of all my questions—"why," "how come"—in my mixture of languages.

So as a toddler you understood and spoke Egyptian, Aramaic, and Hebrew? Amazing.

There's more. Israel was the crossroads of eastern and western cultures down through the ages. If traders or armies wanted to go anywhere, they had to go through Israel. And, of course, they brought their languages with them. So as I grew older I learned Greek and Latin as well.

You excelled in everything, didn't you? Was there anything you couldn't do? Of course, you were the so-called Son of God.

Sorry. I should back off.

No, that's okay. I can handle it.

Regardless, let me try that again. Because you had a thirst for knowledge even as a child, and you seemed to excel beyond your years, were you difficult to raise? Did you give Mary and Joseph a difficult time trying to contain your enthusiasm?

I did everything my parents wanted me to do. In fact, I often anticipated their words and their actions. I did the right things. I never did the wrong things. It sounds precocious, doesn't it? It was just the way I was. I never even thought of disobeying my parents.

What did your brothers and sisters think of you? You never got in trouble, you always obeyed—come on!

I didn't like it when they got in trouble, when they had to be disciplined. I would cry with them and share their hurt. I played with them, too, and we all stood up for each other. But still, there was some jealousy. Simon, one of my half-brothers, actually got quite angry with me a lot, accusing me of being "Mama's boy." But I never gloated or tried to outdo them.

So you grew up in a normal peasant home. You were a typical boy at times, and quite atypical at other times. What were you like as you got older, in your pre-teen years?

As close to Mary as I was all my childhood years, I wasn't a Mama's boy. Oh, yes, Mary and I had a special relationship. We talked a lot about who I was and what I was to become. In some ways, though, I was closer to Joseph. He was a good man and obeyed the laws of God. I looked up to him and tried to model myself after him. When I was old enough to learn the carpenter's trade, I enjoyed the times that we worked side by side, bringing life into a piece of wood as we talked and laughed and shared.

As a boy I was lean and strong. I climbed all the hills around Nazareth, and I climbed Mount Tabor, which was just across the valley, and Mount Carmel, across the Jezreel Valley. I climbed its rocky slopes many times. I explored the world around me. I liked to run fast and far, feeling the wind blowing in my face. I liked to shout and hear my echo, to laugh and to make the noises that boys make. I enjoyed life…yes…I really enjoyed life.

As a teenager, I did what teens do—having fun, gathering with the other teens when I had time. Believe it or not, even as a teen I obeyed my parents. They never had to discipline me.

And, believe it or not, I enjoyed my studies. Some of my friends didn't like school, but I read everything I could get my hands on. The words came alive as I read them, and in my mind I lived what I read, the works of Moses, the prophets, the psalms. It was as if I already knew the Scriptures. And I did.

Well, you did get in trouble with your parents, didn't you? Like that time in Jerusalem when you were twelve?

Every year Joseph and Mary went to Jerusalem for Passover. I wanted so badly to go with them. Passover was one of my favorite feasts. When I finally got to go I was so excited. I spent as much time as I could in the temple, listening to the teachers and asking them questions. I wanted to absorb everything. The teachers were amazed at how much I knew and the caliber of questions I asked. I knew more than they knew. Believe me, I kept them on their toes!

So you were a smart...smart aleck 12-year-old who thought he knew everything?

You don't have to clean up your language for me.

You knew what I wanted to say?

Yes, and I told you I could handle it. No, I didn't show off or try to make them look foolish. In our society, we honored our elders, especially our teachers. They were older and wiser, and we always deferred to them. But in talking with the teachers in the temple, I couldn't deny within myself who I was or what I knew. One of the teachers there in the temple put his finger on it. At one point he looked me in the eye and said, "You are an extraordinary blend of fun-loving young man and serious adult. Someday you will turn the world upside down." How close he was to the truth!

You got your parents quite concerned, didn't you? You were always off exploring Jerusalem or playing with your friends, so they didn't notice you were missing until they started on their journey back home.

Yes, they were quite concerned. And they should have been. But they didn't understand. During the three days and nights that I was in the temple with the teachers—and there ended up being quite a crowd of them—I didn't even think about my family or eating or sleeping. I lost all track of time. I was in my Father's house, talking with the most learned teachers in Israel about Him. Inwardly I burned with the mission that He had sent me on, to bring His people back to Him. I could hardly wait until He set me free to do what He had called me to.

Okay, back at home...

Back at home, throughout my teen years and twenties, it became more and more difficult for me to keep quiet. I felt compelled to do my Father's work, but it wasn't time yet.

How did you know it wasn't time?

I knew...

I went off by myself quite often, praying to my Father and daydreaming about what would be. I would go for long walks alone. At the same time I didn't shirk my duties as a carpenter or as a provider for the family. Joseph died during these years so the burden of keeping the family intact fell on me.

As you grew older, what did your brothers and sisters feel about you?

They didn't understand me. I was an enigma to them. They didn't feel what I felt, my zeal for the things of God, my restlessness, my quietness. I was a stranger in my own home.

Mary and I still talked a lot. Though I was a puzzle to her much of the time, she seemed to understand. She knew I was special. She never forgot how God's Holy Spirit overshadowed her, and the angel told her that I would be Savior of our people.

You were into your late 20s and still living at home. Most people would have given up on that promise years before.

No…Mary never gave up. You see, most priests began their ministry when they turned 30. So she expected I would begin my ministry at that age. Shortly after my 30th birthday we attended a wedding a few miles from our hometown. It was a gala party, with dancing and wine and food.

Did you enjoy the party?

Oh, yes. I always enjoyed parties. I enjoyed everything that celebrated life. Late in the evening they ran out of wine. That's when Mary suggested that I do something about it. I told her no, it wasn't the right time.

She pursued, though, didn't she?

Mary knew my heart. She knew it was the right time. She told the servants, "Do whatever he tells you."

So you…?

…turned the water in six 20-gallon stone jars into wine.

From that moment on, things were different. I was no longer Mary's child. It was time to give myself to my creation, to share with the world how much I loved them. The wedding was the turning point, the sign that I had arrived on the stage of human history.

You brought new life to the party.

Yes! And that's what I was all about—new life, glorious and abundant life for all who believed in me!

Was that your first miracle?

Yes. Most of the people at the wedding didn't know I had done anything. But some of them complemented the wine steward on how good the wine was. The best they had ever tasted.

What happened next?

After the wedding I began preaching and healing throughout that whole region. I told the people the good news about God's Kingdom. And I healed every kind of disease and sickness, even people who were crippled and blind and tormented by demons. The people had never seen anyone like me. They came from everywhere and began to follow me, from the Galilee to Jerusalem and even up north close to Damascus and over to Tyre and Sidon and from the Mediterranean to the other side of the Jordan. Everyone was trying to touch me, because power was going out from me and healing all who came to me.

The news about me had spread to Nazareth, where I grew up. When I went home one weekend, I attended the meeting on the Sabbath as I had done all my life. During the service the rabbi gave me the scroll of Isaiah to read, where it says "God has chosen me to tell the good news to the poor, to announce freedom for prisoners, to give sight to the blind, to free everyone who suffers, and to proclaim 'This is the year God has chosen.'"

Everyone in the service (actually everyone in town) was so proud. I was one of their own. "He's a son of Joseph!" they said. "One of our own has made good." They crowded around, all smiles and happiness.

But I didn't accept their praise. They weren't praising me. They were proud of their new bragging rights about the hometown boy. I went right to the heart of the matter. "You might praise me now," I told them. "But in time you won't believe me. You won't accept me. I tell you, you must love your neighbors right here in Nazareth as you love yourselves. You must forgive others, as God forgives you. You must stop cheating others, stop gossiping about them. You must change, from within. You must let God, Himself, make you clean and set you free. He has sent me to proclaim this. To proclaim that you are the ones Isaiah is talking about—the poor, the blind, the prisoners. You must believe in me as the Son of God. But you won't. No prophet is accepted in his hometown."

They became so angry that they threw me out of town. They dragged me to the edge of a cliff with huge sharp boulders all the way down. They wanted to throw me over the side to kill me. You see, the people of this world hated me, because I told them about the evil things they thought and did. This hatred was to follow me all my life.

So what happened?

I slipped away. They were so caught up in their rage, they didn't even notice for awhile.

Why did you make the people angry? If you were, and are, the Son of God, aren't you love and peace and kindness?

Oh, yes, yes. I am love and peace and kindness and forgiveness and hope. I am life. I am also truth. Let me tell you this, people can't experience a change in their life until they are faced with the truth. You cannot experience my love and forgiveness until you acknowledge the truth that you have fallen short of my standards, that you need to repent of your sins, that you need to seek me with all your being, and that I will forgive you of everything you have ever done.

Believe me, I will forgive all the hurts you have caused to other people, all the wrong thoughts that have ever gone through your mind, if you let me. I am not delusional. I don't pat you on the back and say it's okay, when it's not.

So the crux of what I taught and lived was that I love you with a love that is far beyond any human emotion. But you've got to recognize your faults, your sins, and ask me to forgive you of them, before you can truly experience my love. I was always digging down to the bedrock of people's lives, exposing their sins, then providing forgiveness and hope.

Wow! You've said a mouthful. Sin, forgiveness. We've got to talk about that. But I've got to know how and why the people you grew up with reacted to you. Did your family hate you?

They didn't hate me, no, but they turned against me. They were embarrassed. They thought I was making a fool of myself. Mary knew who I was and why I had come. My brothers and sisters didn't understand. But generally they kept their thoughts to themselves.

Why didn't they understand?

They had known me all their lives. They knew there was something different about me as we grew up together—my zeal for the things of God, the many times when I would go off by myself to pray and meditate, the fact that I would spend more time talking with adults than playing with the other kids. To my brothers and sisters, I was just "different."

More than that, though, some well-known religious leaders came to Nazareth and stirred up the family. They claimed that I was under the power of the devil and everything I said and did was demonic.

That's something else we have to talk about. The devil, or Satan, or whatever…

We'll get there. But let me tell you more about these religious leaders. When I left Nazareth and went to another town on the shores of Lake Galilee, these hate mongers followed me, continuing to stir up the people. When they saw how popular I was becoming, they sent word back to Nazareth, urging my mother and brothers to come and take me home, by force if need be. They planted the seed that I was mentally disturbed, deranged, even dangerous.

One night one of my disciples invited me to his house for dinner. The townspeople heard about it, and they came and just walked in. They filled the house so that we couldn't even eat. My family chose this night to come for me. They couldn't get inside the house because of the crowds, so they passed the word that they were outside and wanted to talk with me.

Now, I loved my family. I was very close to Mary, and I really cared for my half brothers and sisters, even though they didn't understand. But I wanted to diffuse the situation—I knew why they had come—and I wanted to use this occasion to teach about God's family. I looked around at everybody in the house and I asked, who is my mother and who are my brothers and sisters? You are…if you obey God.

My family went home empty handed, the leaders were defeated, and my popularity continued to spread. When the people saw me heal obviously sick and maimed people, and when they heard my message of love and saw how I lived out that message every day, there was no way they would believe that I was a mental case or under the power of the devil.

What a turbulent ministry you had! Those in power hated you and hounded you day after day, but the common people loved you.

You know, that was predicted in the Scriptures hundreds of years before I came on the scene. One of the prophets foretold that I would be despised and rejected, that I would be a man of sorrows and acquainted with grief. And that's exactly the way it was. I caused problems, I upset the social order by spending time with the so-called riff raff, the outcasts of society. I called the leaders hypocrites, and I forgave the sins of prostitutes. Of course they despised and rejected me. They didn't know the truth of God. They were the blind leading the blind.

And so it is today. No matter how brilliant the natural man may be, no matter how cultured, educated, devout, or sincere, he is utterly unable to know the things of God. But when he is born again, and his spiritual eyes are opened, then he understands spiritual things. That's when life begins to make sense.

You see, I came to give people that kind of life, and to give it to them abundantly.

Did you ever get angry?

Did you ever get angry? Did you laugh? Did you cry?

Yes, I got angry. I was angry at all the buying and selling going on in the temple and the charging of exorbitant prices by people whose only motive was to get rich at the expense of others. People came from all over the world to worship there. It was my Father's temple. People came to worship *Him*! Merchants and money changers and temple officials turned it into a marketplace. What kind of worship is that?

Then there was the man with the withered hand. It was the Sabbath, the day of worship. I told the man to stand up so everyone could see him. Most of the people in the congregation knew the man and wanted him to be healed. I wanted to heal him. But there were so-called "influential" people there who were ready to condemn me if I did. After all, it was against the religious law to "work" on the Sabbath. I was angry as I looked around at them. They were so stubborn, so "righteous." No one said a word. I looked those "righteous" people in the eye, then I looked at the man. I told him, "Stretch out your hand." He did, and his withered hand was instantly healed. Everyone saw it happen. I didn't care what they thought. The man needed the use of both hands to make a living. He believed I could do it. So I healed him.

Another time I got angry—exasperated really—when there was a boy who had terrible bouts of epilepsy. His seizures would throw him into fires and into water. He was scared that someday the seizures would kill him. This particular time I wasn't there when the seizure got hold of him. A crowd of people pushed my disciples into trying to heal him. The crowd wanted to see a circus act, to see the "funny" boy healed. Of course my disciples couldn't heal him. I knew the situation immediately when I arrived.

"Don't you people have any faith?" I asked firmly. "How much longer must I be with you? I'm not here to do circus acts. I'm here to make people whole and functional, not to perform magic. Why do I have to put up with you?"

I had them bring the boy to me. I healed him. Quietly, no drama. No more seizures, no more fear, no more taunting and laughing. End of story.

You always seemed so serious. Did you enjoy life? Did you laugh, did you have fun?

Of course I laughed. Every normal person laughs.

But nowhere in the Gospels does it say that you laughed.

That's right, and nowhere in the Gospels does it say that I took a bath, or washed my face, or brushed my teeth. But I assure you I did. You know, I was like most people. I enjoyed breakfast on the beach and sailing on the lake and walking through the fields on a summer evening. Most of all I enjoyed people. Talking with them and listening to them. Sharing their sorrows and encouraging them. I was—and still am—a people person.

I loved a good party. Remember, I performed my first miracle at a wedding party. I enjoyed social functions with tax collectors and other so-called "sinners." The story I told about the prodigal son was a sad story, but it ended with a party. The son had come home!

I enjoyed getting on my hands and knees and playing with little children. You should have heard them giggle. They would dance and play their games, and I'd laugh and clap my hands. They'd clamber onto my lap and look at me with their big trusting eyes until we laughed together. Then I would tell them stories, and we would laugh some more.

You weren't a holier-than-thou kind of person, were you?

No. I was a down-to-earth, easy-going, fun guy. The problem is that even today people find it difficult to think that I did normal, everyday things. I was a joyful person, and I was always urging my followers to be joyful. Oh, I could get angry, but only when the occasion called for it.

Did you cry?

Yes. Many times. I cried when I looked at Jerusalem and all the missed opportunities her people had because they didn't understand me or why I had come to them. I cried when Judas left the room that night at the last supper, knowing that he was going to betray me. I cried when Peter denied me. I cried when Mary and Martha told me that Lazarus had died. I cried, oh, I cried that last night in the garden when I was praying to my Father.

I had emotions. I got angry at injustice. I wept with those who were grieving. And yet I experienced tremendous joy in life. I was no gloom-and-doom guy. My goodness! Life is precious, and you've got to live it to the fullest.

How did you react when people came running after you wherever you went?

My heart went out to them. They were like sheep without a shepherd. I wanted to become their shepherd, to share God's love with them.

There was one day when 5,000 men, and more than that because of all the women and children, sat on a hillside in the sun from morning 'til sunset, listening to my teaching about God's Kingdom. They were getting quite hungry. There was nowhere to buy food because we weren't even close to a town.

So I said to my disciples, "Does anybody in the crowd have food they could share? Go and see."

So they did, and they found a boy who was willing to share his dinner of two small fish and five little loaves of bread. I blessed the food and told my disciples to give it to the people to eat. They looked at me like, well, like I had been in the sun too long. But they did it. You know the outcome. Everyone ate as much as they wanted, and there were 12 baskets of fish and bread pieces left over.

You were compassionate, weren't you? And you were patient?

That's exactly what love is—compassionate, patient, understanding. When people are hungry, they need to be fed.

But you weren't always so compassionate, were you? Later in your ministry you told your disciples that you would be killed then come back to life three days later.

Peter rebuked you for saying that and tried to correct you, didn't he?

Yes, but I had to correct him. Love sometimes involves correction, discipline. What's one of your phrases today—"tough love?"

I said, "Peter, you're thinking like everyone else. You're not thinking like God."

I knew the suffering and pain I would have to endure, that I would be tortured and killed. It was God's plan that these things should happen, and I knew it.

Peter had to learn the hard way.

When you talked, did you sound like God? I mean were your words measured, you know, formal, or did you talk just like us, like them?

What does God sound like? Like the thunder? Like the wind in the trees? I talked the way you talk. But let me say this, I spoke with authority. I knew what I was talking about. I knew what people needed to hear, and I spoke to those needs. I wasn't wishy-washy. I didn't play games. I looked people in the eye, and I said what needed to be said.

Could someone tell that you were God just by looking at you?

Same question, same answer. What does God look like? Does He have a beard? Does He wear designer clothes? No, God is a spirit. He is what He is. I am what I am. I looked like a human. I lived like a human. I ate, I slept, I got sore feet when I walked, I got hungry and thirsty, my clothes got dirty, the wind blew my hair. I had bad hair days.

I was human in every way. At the same time, I was God…In every way, I was God.

Tell me about your disciples.

Did you ever lust after a woman?

No, I never did. I was a man, yes, and tempted just like all men are tempted. And women, too. But I couldn't have done what I was sent to do if I had let myself be sidetracked by physical relationships. I had to keep focused on what I was here for.

I had some wonderful friendships with women. I was very close to my mother, Mary. Two of my best friends were Martha and her sister, Mary. There were other women—Joanna, Salome, Mary Magdalene, Susanna—who were very dear to me. And other remarkable women, too, like the woman who had suffered with the flow of blood for 12 years, the woman who had been crippled for 18 years, completely bent over and not able to straighten up, the woman caught in adultery, and the woman who washed my feet with her tears. What faith they all had! But if I had lusted after any of them, it would have absolutely destroyed what I was here to do.

Yes, I was tempted in many ways, just as you are. That was the human part of my nature. But I couldn't give in to whatever the temptation was. I couldn't sin, because that was totally opposed to my nature as God.

Let me put it this way. As God, as Creator, I loved women—and men—with a far greater love than you could ever imagine. It wasn't a lustful "love." It was much more than that. I cared for people, I embraced them, I accepted them for who they were. I was the road map to what they could be. I could not, I would not, destroy this by dwelling on a selfish, fleshly desire.

I guess you've already answered this next question, but I've got to ask. Did you ever want to get married?

No. I was here on my Father's business. I had only a short time, and I had to make the most of it. The Kingdom of God was at hand. It was imminent; it was here. I had to stay focused on what the Father sent me here for.

Okay, let's go on to something else. You mentioned that women were among your followers. So, you weren't a solo act, traveling from town to town doing your preaching and healing? There were people who followed you, "disciples" I think they were called?

My followers included both men and women. Many of them traveled with me wherever I went. Most of them, however, couldn't leave their homes or employment so they were only with me when I went to their towns. I've already mentioned some of the women. Mary Magdalene, Mary the mother of James and Joseph, and Salome had been my disciples throughout my ministry. Also Susanna and Joanna.

You've heard me talk about some of the men who followed me—Joseph of Arimathea, Nicodemus, the Roman centurion, and, of course, the Twelve closest to me—Peter, James and John, Andrew, Philip, Bartholomew, James the son of Alphaeus, Judas, Matthew, Simon the Zealot, Thaddaeus, and Thomas.

Joseph and Nicodemus were members of the Jewish national assembly and were there when that council condemned me to death. The Chief Priest and his followers were determined to see me killed. Nicodemus spoke up in defense of me in front of the entire body, but it did no good. He was laughed out of court, in a sense. Joseph went to the Roman Governor Pilate after I was crucified and asked for my body so he could bury it properly in his own tomb. Joseph and Nicodemus both anointed me with spices—actually Nicodemus brought 75 pounds of spices—and they wrapped me in grave clothes and laid me in Joseph's new, unused tomb.

That's another story and we'll get to it. But going back to the women—

You have a one-track mind, don't you? As I said, women were among my disciples. You can search the ancient writings from cover to cover, and you won't find anybody else at that time who had close female followers.

Why?

In most cultures back then, women were property, one of many possessions that a man might have. In a sense, women were just a step above slaves. They had no money of their own, nothing they could call their own. They were not even supposed to associate with men they were not related to. But I respected women. Men *and* women are equal in God's eyes.

Let me tell you about one of the women who became one of my disciples. She was a prostitute and, in fact, had made a lot of money in that "profession." One of the religious leaders, a man well respected in the community, invited me to dinner. Simon was a smart, cunning lawyer. He had hired this woman to hide in an upstairs room, then at his signal to come down and ensnare me in a compromising moment.

He had planned his elaborate "trap" very carefully. When I arrived, the party was well under way. All the guests were cronies of Simon. They were to be his witnesses.

Simon was somewhat standoffish. He didn't want to compromise himself by getting too close to me. He didn't greet me with a kiss on my cheek, as is the Middle Eastern custom. He didn't provide water to wash the dust off my feet. He didn't pour olive oil on my head, which was a kind of socially acceptable "anointing."

During dinner Simon continually tried to confound me with his crafty religious arguments. He wanted to set the stage by getting me flustered and confused. I saw through his arguments and came back with questions of my own that stumped him. So the meal went.

This "debate" was interrupted by the arrival of the woman. She was holding a bottle of expensive perfume. As she stood on the stairs, looking at me, her eyes filled with tears. Then, weeping profusely, she knelt at my feet (in those days we reclined on couches while eating, rather than sitting in chairs), and began to anoint my feet with the perfume. After she had massaged my feet, she dried them with her long hair, kissing my feet at the same time.

Simon was speechless. This wasn't the plan. He screamed at me. "Don't you know who this woman is? She's a whore!"

I stared at him. As he calmed down, I asked him to think about this: A moneylender had two debtors. One owed him a thousand shekels, the other a hundred shekels. Neither debtor could pay his debt, but the moneylender forgave them both. The question I asked Simon was, which of the two debtors was the more grateful? Simon replied it must have been the debtor who had owed the most.

"When I entered your house," I told him, "you gave me no water for my feet. But she has washed my feet with her tears and wiped them with her hair. You greeted me with no kiss, but she has not ceased to kiss my feet. You did not anoint my head with olive oil, but she has anointed my feet with expensive perfume. So, Simon, I tell you, her sins, which are many, are forgiven."

Simon just stood there, mouth open, not saying anything. He knew what I was saying.

I helped the woman to her feet and looked into her eyes. "Your faith has made you clean. Go in peace."

I'm sorry. I shouldn't have taunted you. Let's talk more about the men who were your disciples.

No, let's continue talking about the women, since you brought it up.

Another one of my female disciples was Joanna, wife of Herod Antipas' estate manager. Herod Antipas was the son of Herod the Great. Remember him? He was King when I was born and had all those babies murdered. Thirty years later this son of his ordered the beheading of my cousin, John.

Because Joanna's husband was a high official, she was able to pretty much do what she wanted. She not only followed me around Galilee, along with all my other disciples, she supported me financially to help pay for food and other expenses. She had access to her husband's wealth and used it to help my ministry. Now, this was dangerous. She not only stepped out of her social circle, but left her home from time to time to follow me, and put her husband's career at risk by doing so. After all, I had publicly insulted her husband's boss by calling him "that fox," referring to Herod's murderous character.

Herod Antipas didn't like me, but he was too afraid of the people to do anything. He was waiting for the right time. And it came. Just three years later.

You had 12 disciples that were kind of an "inner core." What were they like?

These were wonderful men! A person couldn't have better friends. They came in all shapes and sizes. Some were balding, some short and portly, some tall and slim, some older, some younger, some with beards, some impulsive, some patient and thoughtful, some who accepted the Roman occupation and some who were staunchly anti-Rome, some skilled in languages, some who spoke only Aramaic, some muscular, some well-to-do, some poor, some belligerent, some outspoken, some quiet. There were jealousies, arguments, pettiness, squabbles. But I really enjoyed being around these guys.

And you loved them?

Oh, yes. All of them.

Tell me about them. Peter, for example.

Peter was quite a guy. Big, muscular, impulsive, outspoken without thinking first. He made me smile a lot. I was proud of him when he made the right choices. But when he was wrong…I had to reprove him more than any other disciple. He obeyed easily and reacted passionately, but when he lost his focus he failed miserably.

Like the time he scrambled over the side of the boat to meet me as I walked by. He paid no attention to what he was doing and was almost to me when he realized what was happening. He sank like a rock! I couldn't help laughing. I reached out and grabbed him. He was sputtering and thrashing about. He had a lot to learn about faith.

Or the time we ate our last meal together. To teach the Twelve a lesson on humility and servanthood, I was washing their feet. Peter couldn't handle this. He said, "Lord, you're not going to wash *my* feet! Do you know how worthy you are and how unworthy I am?"

Oh, Peter! All this time together and he didn't know who I was.

"Peter," I said calmly to him, "you don't know what I'm doing, but you'll understand later."

He roared, "You'll never wash my feet!"

"If I don't wash you," I told him, "you don't really belong to me."

"Lord," he bellowed even louder, not missing a beat, "Don't wash just my feet. Wash my hands and my head."

I had tears in my eyes when he said that.

What did you think when Peter denied you?

I knew he would deny me, and I knew he would return.

"Simon," I said, "I have prayed that your faith will be strong. When you come back to me, help the others."

But still I was hurt. I knew that he would deny me three times that night. You see, I know what all men are going to do or think even before they know. I know when they're going to make the wrong choices, when they're going to think the wrong thoughts, when they're going to fool themselves into believing they know better than anyone else knows. When I created mankind, I gave them free will to make those choices, to think that way. Even so, I feel the pain when they do.

I knew that Peter would go on to become a leader—a strong, bold, fearless leader—who would make the right choices. And he did. But what a struggle it was to get to that point.

What about Simon the Zealot? I mean, you called fishermen, tax collectors, intellectuals, even doubters to be among the Twelve. Why did you call an out-and-out rebel to be one of your closest followers?

At the beginning of this interview, you called me a rebel, a revolutionary. I wasn't a rebel in the sense that Simon was. I've already told you a little bit about him. He was what you would call a guerrilla, a "paramilitary religious fanatic." The bottom line was that he was a terrorist. He had killed people.

My questions still stands. Why did you choose him to be one of your inner circle?

Would you believe because I loved him?

No.

Well, you better reconsider. Love is the greatest force in the world. Love has saved more people in the history of the world than military might has ever killed. When Simon came into my fold, his fiery patriotism turned into a deep and lasting zeal for me and my mission. What a transformation! Where hatred had ruled his life, love took over. I could go on and on about Simon. He was an important part of my ministry while I was on earth and an exceedingly powerful witness after I left to return to my Father.

Okay, now let me ask you a tough one. What about Judas?

What about him?

Why was he one of your twelve disciples? Why did you choose him? How did you feel about him? Did you

know that he would betray you? Did you love him like you loved the others?

You're wound up on that one, aren't you? Did I love him? Yes. Did I love him as much as I loved the other disciples? Most emphatically, yes! Simon and Judas came to me together. They were both Zealots. They both thought that I was the answer to their dreams, that I was going to be the political answer to the problem of the Romans. Both of them participated zealously (pun intended!) in my ministry.

Did I know that Judas would betray me? Yes, even before Judas knew.

There was one time when I sent the Twelve to every town in that area. I told them not to take anything with them, not even a walking stick or a traveling bag or a change of clothes or food or money. (Can you imagine Judas not worrying about money? But he didn't, not at this stage of his life.) So they left, all twelve of them, and went from village to village, telling about God's Kingdom and healing people everywhere. Even Judas told the good news and healed people in my name.

It was later that Judas became quite money centered. He kept the money bag for us and would take money for himself when he thought no one was looking. When Mary, Lazarus' sister, anointed me with expensive perfume, Judas complained that the perfume should have been sold and the money given to the poor. He wasn't concerned about the poor. He had lost his focus. No longer was the Zealot movement or his relationship with me his consuming passion. All he cared about was money, about satisfying his own needs.

Could anyone be your disciple?

I personally chose the Twelve. But in the larger sense, anyone could follow me. I had stipulations, however. I told them "You cannot be my disciple unless you love me more than you love your father and mother, your wife and children, and your brothers and sisters. You cannot come with me unless you love me more than you love your own life. You cannot be my disciple unless you carry your own cross and come with me." I meant that. Some dropped out because it was too demanding, but most stayed with me. Until the end, that is, when I was arrested and condemned to death. Only a few stayed with me then.

How did you die?

After three years of intense ministry, were you close to burning out?

"Burning out" isn't the word. Tired, yes. Discouraged, yes. Ready for it to be over, yes. Don't get me wrong. I enjoyed what I was doing so very much. I had a passion to reach out to people, to heal them, to care for them, to put my arm around them and love them. But still…

The pressure was intense. Crowds followed me everywhere. Those who didn't like me were always trying to trap me in one argument or another. They thought that if they could prove me false in one area, they could prove me false in every area. I was continually trying to teach my disciples, but they often didn't understand.

I didn't get a lot of sleep. People crowded around me all day long. At night I didn't get to sleep until quite late, and I got up early. Sometimes I stayed up all night, praying to my Father.

I needed those times, just to be alone with Him and talk with Him.

In truth, sleep wasn't that important. I had a job to do, and I had to keep at it until it was finished. Spending time with my Father and the people He sent me to was important. Very important.

You said earlier in this interview that you were arrested and condemned to death. Why?

There were three reasons, all of them centered around the fact that I was a threat to the religious establishment.

First, I was popular.

How can you say that with a straight face?

You asked me a question. I'm answering it.

People began to pay more attention to me than to the leaders. The religious and political leaders craved attention. They lived for the adoration and praise people gave them. When people began following me, hanging onto my every word, applauding everything I did and said, it infuriated the leaders.

I fired up the imaginations of the people. I was someone new, exciting, different—healing and teaching and spending time with them. I didn't have the superior attitude the leaders had. I was approachable, someone people could laugh with and be friends with.

Reason number two?

I undermined their authority. The religious leaders prided themselves on setting the standards of conduct, of right and wrong, what was socially acceptable and unacceptable. Me? I quoted a Higher Authority and held people to a different standard. My standards were based on love, rather than on some kind of man-made law.

70

The religious leadership especially didn't like it when I rode into Jerusalem that last Sunday like a king, with crowds of people waving palm branches and laying down their cloaks before me. The leaders had been against me from the very beginning, trying to turn the people against me, accusing me falsely, saying I healed through the power of the devil, that I was filled with demons, that I was crazy. They tried to trap me in all kinds of religious and legal questions, tax questions, authority questions. They called me a wine bibber and a glutton, a "party boy." They berated me for spending time with "foreigners" and "riff raff."

I called them "hypocrites," because they said one thing and did something else. Everything they did was for show. They piled heavy burdens on people's shoulders but didn't lift a finger to help. They showed absolutely no love, no mercy, no forgiveness.

I told them to their faces that they, as religious "leaders," didn't know what the Scriptures taught about the will of God. I told them unequivocally there will be a final judgement and that those who don't commit their life to me will go to hell and those who do will spend eternity with me in heaven.

Number three?

Blasphemy.

"Are you the Son of the glorious God?" they asked me.

"Yes, I am," I replied, looking directly at them. "Soon you will see me sitting at the right side of God Almighty, and coming with the clouds of heaven."

They couldn't stand this. The High Priest ripped his robe and shouted, "You heard what He said. This man must be put to death for impersonating God!"

Today you wouldn't be put to death for being popular, or for speaking with authority, or for claiming to be God.

I would be. The charges would be different, but the result would be the same.

So how did they go about convincing the Romans that you should be killed?

You're right that only the Romans could declare the death penalty. To get Rome to bring about my death, the religious leaders had to convince the authorities that it was in their best interest.

They had plotted to kill me on numerous occasions. They couldn't make up their minds, however, on the official reason. Whatever the outcome, the religious leaders had to come out of it looking good.

At first they thought they could charge me with sedition. You know, subversive activity, because Zealots were part of my inner circle. But that didn't go over too well, because some of the Jewish leaders had a pretty cozy relationship with the Romans, themselves, and they didn't want that to end.

Then they thought they could get rid of the evidence, primarily Lazarus. My raising him from the dead was the reason many people were turning to me. If they could discredit this miracle, maybe they could discredit me and the people would become confused and disillusioned in me. It was a long shot, but they had to counter my popularity.

It didn't work, did it?

They didn't even try. Too many people had seen it happen, and the leaders thought it would boomerang and make them look bad.

So how did they go about arresting you?

They finally settled on the blasphemy charge. You see, Israel was a theocracy—

Where religion and the state are intertwined?

That's right. My Father set it up that way when He told Abraham that his descendants would be His chosen people.

So blasphemy was a pretty serious offense?

The most serious offense. The leaders reasoned that Rome would understand that religion was so important to the nation of Israel, and that I was destroying that foundation, and it would be better for me to be killed than for the entire nation to perish.

So the plan was that they would arrest me when I came to Jerusalem for the high festival. During that week, the city would be thronged shoulder to shoulder with people from all over Israel. The religious leaders would command the people to tell them if anyone saw me. They would even offer money as a reward.

I had told the Twelve several times about my coming death and resurrection. I told them that I would be handed over to foreigners who would make fun of me, mistreat me, spit on me.

"They will beat me and kill me," I told them, "but three days later I will come back to life."

The Twelve didn't listen. They didn't want to believe that I was going to die.

On our way to Jerusalem for the high festival, some of the religious leaders who were secretly my followers warned me, "Stay away from Jerusalem! Herod wants to kill you."

As much as I appreciated their warning, I said to them, "I've got three more days before that fox will try to kill me. During that time I've got a lot to do. You tell him this—I know what's going to happen, and I'm not worried about him."

My death was inevitable. It was God's plan.

By the end of the week, Judas had made a deal with the authorities to "betray" me. The religious leaders were elated. Here was one of my own disciples, one of my inner circle, selling me out. Judas bargained for double what they were offering, but the leaders rejoiced in their good fortune. *How easy this was going to be!*

What happened next?

That night in a garden across the valley from Jerusalem, I prayed all night. I knew what was going to happen. I could already feel the pain, the torture that I would be suffering. I didn't want to be alone, so I asked the Eleven to keep watch with me. But they fell asleep...

They fell asleep...even as I cried deep gut-wrenching sobs in my prayer to the Father. Sweat poured from my body...mixed with blood...I...I didn't want to go through with it.

I cried out, "Father, please take this cup from me...please, please, please..."

But I knew I had to die. It was the Father's will.

"Father, Your will be done...not what I want...but what You want..."

Judas led the soldiers to me in the garden. He kissed me on the cheek as the sign that I was the one they had come for. My disciples ran away.

All night long they questioned me, first the Chief Priest, then Roman Governor Pilate, finally King Herod. I kept quiet. There was nothing to say. Soldiers blindfolded me and mocked me, spit on me, struck me in the face. They even tore out part of my beard.

Early the next morning, exhausted from a sleepless night, my body clothed in pain, I was taken back to Pilate. As cruel as he was, he didn't want me crucified. He didn't think it was justified. But he had me beaten with a whip. He thought that would satisfy everyone.

What was it like, the beating?

Do you really want me to tell you? The short version is that it was brutal, sadistic.

I want a sense of what you went through.

Okay, but it's graphic.

First, I was stripped of my clothing, stripped of my dignity. My hands were tied to a post above my head. A Roman soldier beat me with a whip of leather thongs with pieces of sharp bone braided into the ends. He used his full force as he beat me across my shoulders, my back, my buttocks, the back of my legs.

Again…and again…and again.

I don't know how many lashes…39…40…I didn't count…

The thongs cut through my skin…then deeper into my muscles. I could feel the blood flowing down my back…dripping onto my ankles and onto the dusty ground…

Then, still mocking me—they were having great fun doing this—soldiers threw a purple robe around me over the wounds and pushed a "crown" of inch-long thorns onto my head. I couldn't see through the blood that matted my hair and worked its way down my face. Then they tore the robe off me…strips of my flesh and semi-dried blood hanging from it…

Finally they threw my clothes over me…covering my nakedness…

Do you want more?

Yes.

Beating didn't satisfy the crowd. They wanted crucifixion. I had healed many of them, their relatives, their friends. I had taught them about God's love. I had laughed with them and cried with them and had become a friend to them. But they wanted crucifixion.

I was standing there, totally exhausted, bloody, in excruciating pain, depleted. I was Pilate's pawn.

"Whom shall I set free?" he challenged the crowd. "The murderer Barabbas or Jesus?"

It was tradition that someone would be freed from prison during the festival.

"Barabbas!" the crowd roared. Again and again, louder and louder—"Barabbas!"

That surprised Pilate. He couldn't believe they wanted the murderer set free and the innocent one crucified. But he gave the order, washed his hands of the whole affair, and walked back into his chambers.

I was forced to carry the cross beam, which weighed about a hundred pounds. I staggered maybe 50 yards, then crumpled to the ground with the cross beam partially on top of me. They commanded a bystander, Simon from North Africa, to carry the beam the rest of the way while I was forced to my feet and half stumbled, half walked with the thorns still digging into my scalp.

The soldiers offered me wine mixed with vinegar to dull the pain. I refused. They took the beam from Simon, threw it onto the ground, tore my clothes off me again because criminals were crucified naked, and threw me down on top of the beam...

They pounded a heavy, square, iron nail...5 to 7 inches long...through the wrist of each hand into the already blood-soaked wood of the cross beam. At one time the spikes had a sharp point...but after all the criminals they had nailed to crosses...the points were blunt...and rusty.

They lifted the cross beam with me on it...and nailed it into a notch on the upright already in its hole in the ground. Then my feet...they hammered a spike through each foot into the upright beam...

I was crucified on a gnarled six foot length of what had been an olive tree...my feet just inches off the ground. Passers by could look me almost directly in the face...and stare at me...spit at me...whatever they wanted.

My shoulders were pulled out of their joints as my body hung there. When I let my body sag, it put more weight...on the spikes...in my wrists...and...and...excruciating...pain... shot through my hands...up my arms...exploding in my brain.

I was close to death because of the beating...And even closer to death hanging on that tree...

But still...

the pain...

the pain...

...I can still feel it.

When I pushed upward, my full weight was placed on the spikes in my feet with burning, pulsating pain. Eventually I could push no more, and as I sagged my muscles were paralyzed. I could draw air into my lungs...but I could barely...exhale.

The blood that hadn't coagulated from the wounds in my scalp got into my eyes and rolled down my cheeks. Flies were attracted to the blood. I had flies in my eyes and in my ears and in my nostrils. I couldn't do anything to swipe them away.

Flies. Gnats. Sweat. Pain.

Struggling for breath...I felt searing pain from the open wounds in my back rubbing against the rough wood.

Soldiers took my clothes—sandals, belt, robe, under garment. They didn't care much for the belt and under garment. But they gambled for them anyway to pass the time. The sandals and the robe—that was something else.

The high priests and their followers continued to make fun of me. The soldiers continued to mock. I guess the sight of a person slowly being tortured to death on a cross wasn't enough. They made fun of my nakedness. They taunted me about what a weak, puny God I was.

I saw their eyes...eyes of condemnation...hatred...judgement...rage. Eyes that looked crazed and glossed over. I saw fear in their eyes, fear of what was happening to a man who just days before was welcomed with palm branches and celebration.

Some of my followers stood off to the side, disappointment on their faces. More than disappointment. Hurt, anguish, suffering. My mother and several other women—Susanna, Joanna, Salome, and Mary Magdalene—were so faithful. Then John came and put his arm around my mother, staying near me 'til the end.

They gave me a sponge soaked in sour wine to ease the pain. I tasted it and spat it out. I had to experience the pain. I had to experience the weight of the sins of my people.

My heart began to beat erratically. My breathing almost nonexistent...

After six hours, with little more than a tortured whisper, I said my last words, "It is finished...Father...Forgive them...They don't know what they're doing...Into your hands...I commend my spirit..."

Just before nightfall, the soldiers used the shafts of their spears to shatter the lower leg bones of the two criminals crucified with me to hasten their death. They didn't break my legs. It was obvious that I was already dead. They were professional soldiers. They knew when a man was dead. One of them drove his spear between my ribs into my heart as an afterthought.

If there had been an autopsy, it would have been determined that I died not of suffocation, but of heart failure. Cardiac arrest. A broken heart.

You didn't stay dead, did you?

I'm sorry you had to go through that.

It had to be. I didn't come into human history just to tell you to how to live. I came to provide the way for you to live abundantly and eternally, to live the way my Father wants you to live. Do you understand that?

I don't know. I want to understand it, to believe it. But I still have questions.

You should know by now that I'm not afraid of questions.

Going back to your death. Could you have gotten off the cross? Could you have come down?

Yes. I could have called in legions of angels to surround me and protect me. I could have wiped out the armies of Rome with just one word. I could have proclaimed myself a glorious king come to save my people from their enemies.

Just like I could have jumped off the pinnacle of the temple, when Satan tempted me those 40 days and nights in the desert, and armies of angels would have kept me from even stubbing my toe. Or I could have turned stones into bread...I was so hungry. I could have ruled over all the nations of the earth. I could have had all of this, with no betrayal, no beatings, no taunting, no cross.

But I didn't give in to those temptations. The love I have for you far surpassed all the suffering I endured.

Is that the end of the story, your dying on the cross?

No. Dying on the cross didn't do anything by itself.

What? Now you're playing games with me.

No, I don't play games. Listen to me. If I had stayed dead, with my body rotting in some grave, what would that have accomplished? Absolutely nothing. Just another religious hotshot getting his 15 minutes of fame, then disappearing off the world's stage.

The kicker is, I didn't stay dead. My body didn't decay. The third day after I was crucified, I came back to life. This body, with gaping holes in its hands and feet, a scalp punctured by thorns, lungs that couldn't get air, its back raw from being whipped—this body with blood drained out of it by that spear thrust to the heart—this mutilated body came back to life. Do you see? That's where the meaning is. That's what gives my death on the cross its power. That's where the meaning of the cross becomes real.

You're not saying anything. Are you okay?

I'm fine...I'm just thinking about what you said.

Okay...let me see if I understand. All you stood for as a human, your teaching, your healing, your caring for people—you did that because you were the Son of God. You came to show us what God is like and how we can connect with Him. Am I right?

Yes. Keep going.

The authorities thought they had silenced you when they killed you. They had gotten rid of this goody-goody trouble maker. But you had the last laugh. You came back to life. You really were the Son of God, weren't you? Everything you said was true, everything you did was true. Even death couldn't stop you.

I didn't have the last laugh. There's no laughing to it. I loved them and died for them. I'm so sad they missed the whole point. I was then, I am today, and I will be forever, the Son of God. Yes, my coming back to life confirmed that everything I said and did was true.

This is the good news, that I died for your sins. I confirmed it by rising from the grave, by defeating death. I met death, I fought death, and I beat death. I took the sting out of death for those who believe in me, who commit their lives to me.

Let me ask you a question. Your disciples were surprised when you rose from the dead, weren't they? You told them several times before it happened that you were going to die and come back to life. But still they weren't expecting it. Why?

Because they didn't listen to what I said. They interpreted instead of just believing. They heard what they wanted to hear and dismissed what they didn't want to hear. Even today that's true. People don't listen to what I'm saying. They read the Scriptures, but they don't understand what they're reading. Then they try to interpret it to agree with their own beliefs or expectations. But it's right there. You need to listen to the words of Scripture. Don't just read the words—listen to them.

So your disciples, the inner circle, stayed back in the city sulking and scared and timid.

Some of the women came to my tomb Sunday morning. Mary Magdalene saw that the tomb was empty, so she ran into the city to tell the Eleven disciples. They thought she was babbling, talking nonsense. She went back to the tomb, not so sure of herself this time. She was crying and saw a gardener and asked him where they had put my body. She didn't recognize that the gardener was me.

When I said, "Mary," her face filled with recognition and awe. She fell to my feet to kiss them with her tears. What she was doing was most appropriate. During my life I hadn't let anyone worship me. Worship is reserved for the Father, I said. But now that I had been resurrected by the Father as the everlasting, all-powerful, holy Son of God, without the mantle of humanity embracing me, I wanted my creation to worship me.

So you accepted her worship?

Oh, yes. But I told her not to touch me.

Why?

She wanted to cling to me, to wrap her arms around my legs and feet and never let go, as though she never wanted to lose me again. She had to learn that I would always be with her. I wanted to take her beyond sight and touch, to help her understand that she could be in my presence without my physical body being there.

It was the same lesson I was to teach Thomas later. In just 40 days I would leave this earth to dwell with my Father in heaven, and during that time I wanted to teach all of my disciples, the Eleven and all the others who still followed me, how to carry on my work when I had left. Mary and Thomas and the other believers would have to learn that they couldn't come into my presence any more with eyes and hands. They would know my presence by faith.

Will humans who live with you in heaven have the same kind of body you have?

Yes.

Hmmm…Okay…I wish I understood…

You will.

You appeared to a lot of people after your resurrection, didn't you?

I appeared to the Eleven several times. I walked and talked with two other disciples for several hours along the road from Jerusalem to the town of Emmaus. I appeared to my half brothers, James and Judas. I appeared to a crowd of more than 500 of my followers in Galilee.

Tell me about James and Judas. What happened when you appeared to them?

I appeared to all my brothers and sisters and my mother. Everything made sense to them finally. Why I behaved the way I did and said the things I said when I was growing up, why I would go off by myself so often, why I exhibited so much compassion for people, why I left home to begin healing and teaching. They finally understood.

How did they feel?

Overcome, overawed, overwhelmed. They had been living with God's Son! And they couldn't see it at the time. After I ascended to heaven, my family and a hundred of my followers were in a room on the second floor of a house in Jerusalem, praying day and night for the Holy Spirit to fill them with His presence and power. They could hardly wait to continue my work on earth.

When that happened, when the Spirit overcame them and filled them and energized them, my brothers began preaching and healing throughout Israel. They couldn't be shut up, because they knew, firsthand, what the good news was.

My brother James became the leader of the Jerusalem church, which was the only church at the time. James was a natural leader, a thoughtful, logical man who provided the stability the new church needed. Things were happening so fast. In just one day over 3000 people committed their lives to me. The Jerusalem church became huge and spilled out into the whole world.

James was the perfect one to lead the fledgling church. In fact, he wrote a tough love kind of letter to those first Christians, telling them how to live as believers. That letter's in the New Testament.

My brother Jude also wrote a letter that's in the New Testament. Dear Jude! It's a difficult letter for a lot of people to understand because he wrote it with passion, just as it flowed from his heart. Jude was quite a man, a lot like Peter. Fiery. Dogmatic. He said it the way it was. He fought fire with fire.

During this interview, you've gone into a lot of detail about your life. Why you did things, what you thought about things. You're a pretty straightforward guy.

I want you to understand who I was and why I came to earth. I want you to understand what I did for you. I want you to believe in me, to put your faith, your hope, your trust in me. I want you to put your life in my hands. In a very real way, you died with me on that cross. I took your sins on me, I took your place. You see, sin leads to death. But I triumphed over death. Death no longer has any power over you when you accept what I did for you.

As I died and was raised to life, never again to die, so you will be raised to life when you die, to live eternally with the Father and me.

I am alive. And because I live, you shall also live.

Why did you go through all this?

What was the real reason you died?

I died to liberate you. To set you free.

To set me free from what?

From sin. Do you know what sin is?

I don't like that word. It's much too negative.

It is negative. It's shorthand for rejection of God, for going against His will, for disobeying Him, for thinking you don't need Him, that you are okay without Him, that you are greater than He is, that you want to do it your way.

There are consequences to sin, consequences to that rejection. I died on the cross to take away those consequences, to reconcile you to God. I suffered so that you might be healed by my wounds.

You've been talking about "God" throughout this interview. Who, or what, is God?

Let me ask you the same question. Who do you think God is?

Before I met you, I never thought much about it. I guess I would have said...God is like a policeman or some kind of judge. He's like Santa Claus or even like my grandfather, a doddering old man with a beard falling asleep in his rocking chair. Or God is like a brick wall...or a cosmic fire alarm...or a cloud of nothingness or something infinite and mysterious and out of this world...someone thought up by primitive cultures to explain the unexplainable...a supernatural figure made in my image. A figment of my imagination.

Do you still believe that?

No. I think that was just intellectual garbage I've been carrying around all my life.

Maybe emotional garbage and cultural garbage as well?

Yeah. And you can add to that environment garbage and ego garbage. All kinds of hang-ups. But I've got to admit you've started me thinking about this God thing.

And what do you think about God now?

I don't know. I kind of like who you were, the things you stood for, what you taught, how you treated people. If God is like you...

He is.

Remember when I said the Father and I are one?

Yes.

We truly are one. I wasn't playing rhetorical games when I said that. When I say "God" I'm referring to the Father and the Son (that's me) and the Holy Spirit. We are one. We are one God who reveal ourselves through three distinct persons.

90

We are not three gods, but three persons—who are one. We are threeness and we are oneness at the same time. I am oneness and threeness at the same time. The Father and the Holy Spirit are each oneness and threeness at the same time.

For example, God is Creator (that's Oneness). The Father is Creator because He gave the command, "Let there be." I am Creator because I did the creating. And the Holy Spirit is Creator because He gave life to what I created. (That's Threeness.) Another example: God became man, I was that man, and I continue to live within believers through the Holy Spirit. (That's Oneness and Threeness.)

So in this interview you sometimes say "Me," and sometimes you say "Father," and sometimes you say "God." Those terms are interchangeable. Is that what you're saying?

Sometimes yes, sometimes no. We are one being with three distinct personalities and three distinct expressions of those personalities. We are unity and diversity at the same time.

Do you understand?

Well...No, I don't.

It's all right to say "no." But I want you to listen to what I'm saying with an open mind. Try not to get hung up on any preconceptions, okay?

Okay. Go on.

God is none of those things you mentioned when you were trying to describe Him. He's real—as real as you are real. He's not a figment of imagination or an invention or an old senile man. He's not a crutch or a death wish or a "get out of Hell" card. God was not made in your image; you were made in His image.

God is Spirit, therefore He has no form. He is not bound by a body as you are. He is also not bound by time as you are. He's not bound by anything. You can't put Him in a box.

At the same time, God is Person and Personal. He thinks, He feels, He enjoys, He loves. He is all that is good, all that is right, all that is beautiful. He is just and fair and impartial and unchanging. He is compassionate, forgiving, ultimate wisdom, absolute purity, absolute perfection, absolute holiness.

He is the one and only Supreme Being, the Highest Intelligence, the Highest Love, the Highest Goodness. All else pales in comparison with Him.

That part I can understand. Tell me more.

There's more, much more, about who God is. This is just a thumbnail sketch.

Tell me more about this Creator stuff.

As Supreme Being, God is the one and only Creator. We (Father, Son, and Holy Spirit) created everything that has ever been created, things you can see and things you can't see, from the smallest particle of energy that your scientists haven't yet discovered to the vastness and complexity of galaxies and universes...

That our scientists also haven't yet fully discovered?

There's so much that you haven't discovered or explored. You've only scratched the surface of God's amazingly complex creation.

Go ahead.

God not only created everything, but He continues to watch over His creation. He doesn't stand back and do nothing. He's very much involved in all He has made.

For example, God created you—

He didn't do a very good job of that one. I know myself, and I'm not what a lot of people think I am. God made a mistake with me.

God did a very good job of making you. He doesn't make junk.

That's kind of a crass way of putting it.

But you understand it, don't you?

Yeah. Your point is well taken.

Regardless of how you feel about yourself, you are beautiful in God's sight. You are special. The human race is the most special of all His creation. And, as I said, He made you in His image. That doesn't mean you look like Him. It means He gave you the capacity to love, to will, to feel, to enjoy, to forgive, to think, to make decisions.

You might think you know yourself, but I know you better than you do. I know you intimately—your thoughts, your desires, your fears, your strengths and weaknesses. I know when you are sincere and when you are phony. I know whether your relationships are genuine or if you're manipulating others for your own desires or gain. I know when you honestly seek me, and when you're merely putting on a show.

I don't know if I like a God who knows all about me.

That's the beautiful part about it. God does know all about you. And because He loves you so much, He's always willing to help, to forgive, to share His life with you, in spite of your moral or ethical shortcomings. In spite of what you think about yourself, God cares about you.

Tell me more about this "Son of God" thing. You've tried explaining it, but I'm confused.

93

Let me ask you a question. If God were to break into human history, if He were to make Himself known to mankind in a tangible way, how would He do it?

I don't know. I'm not God.

First, He *wouldn't* make Himself known to man in some mysterious, alien way. He wouldn't create a puzzle or code or leave hidden clues that only the most intelligent of men could figure out. No. He wouldn't make it difficult. He would do it in a most obvious way. By becoming human, Himself. And that's exactly what He did.

If you want to know what God is like, look at me. I am God in human form. Let me repeat that—if God were to break into human history, if He were to make Himself known to mankind in a tangible way, that is me. The good news is that God did become human. He sent me, the Son, to reveal Himself to mankind.

You said eartlier that you like who I am and you wished God were like me.

Yes.

That's exactly it!

Of my own free will I gave up the riches of heaven, the glory, the majesty, the might, the power, the holiness, the awesomeness, the absolute beauty that belong to God alone. I could have made myself a king or emperor or ruler, but I came to earth in the form of a servant. I became a man and appeared on earth in human likeness.

When you lived on earth, some people said you were a good man, a great teacher. A lot of people knew you and many people admired you. But today the majority of people have no idea who you were. They only know

"Jesus Christ" as a swear word. You mean absolutely nothing to them.

They'd have trouble accepting me as God and as the only way to God, wouldn't they?

How can you say that you are God and the way to God at the same time?

Most people have no problem with the concept of "God." What they have a problem with is me. "Jesus Christ" makes God tangible, personal, something that can be grasped. So, while I am, indeed, God, I point people directly to the fact that God is not some amorphous being, but here, real, personal. Therefore, I am the "way" to God. No one comes to God, the true God, except through me.

Can't I find God through some other belief system? Why do I have to go through you?

Because "finding" God isn't a guessing game or a multiple choice test. I am the way. All other ways to whatever god people are looking for are false. There is only one God, and there is only one way.

Isn't that exceedingly intolerant? Doesn't that make God into a being that is bigoted and close minded? When it comes down to it, wouldn't you agree that there are no pat answers, that everyone finds their own truth?

What if your attitude about me, and me alone, determines your eternal destiny?

I think God is a loving God. I think He accepts us as we are.

I agree. He is a loving God and He does accept you as you are. That's why He gave Himself to you through my death on the cross. He loves you so much that He gave His only Son to die in

95

your place, so that whoever believes in Him, in His Son, will not perish but will have everlasting, true, abundant, happy, fulfilling life. This is not a wimpish God, or an intolerant God, but a God who lays it on the line. He gave so you might receive.

That's the way it is. No ifs, ands, or buts.

No questions?

No. I'm just thinking about what you said.

When you're ready, let me know.

Okay, let's keep going. To be honest with you, one part of me wants to argue about this "only one way" business. I want to shout "why?" I want to put you on the spot. I guess many others have done that, and the outcome wasn't what they expected.

Then there's another part of me that wants to accept what you said and go from there.

Which way do you want to go?

What you say makes a lot of sense. So many people are wrapped up in all kinds of ways and how-to's and stuff like that. They don't ever seem to get anywhere with it. It just doesn't satisfy. They're still hungry, but they don't know what they're hungry for.

I think it's so much simpler to believe in one way. I guess I like things black and white rather than "multiple choice."

Remember I said that I died on the cross to reconcile you to God?

Yes.

Why do you think you need to be reconciled to God?

I don't know. Because of sin, I suppose.

That's right. Have you ever heard of Satan?

Of course. Everyone has. He's evil. The exact opposite of God.

Satan is evil, yes. But he's not the opposite of God. God has no opposite. Evil is the opposite of good, not of God. You cannot equate God and Satan.

Okay…

This is important, so listen to me. We're going to go even deeper for awhile. But I want you to try to understand.

This spiritual stuff has already been difficult for me to understand. You might as well tell me more. Maybe someday it'll make sense.

There are two kingdoms in the spiritual world. There's the kingdom of Darkness, which Satan rules, and the Kingdom of Light, which God rules. The kingdom of Satan is condemnation and death. There is no true love in Satan's kingdom, no true joy or happiness or forgiveness or second chances.

Even so, Satan's kingdom is very attractive to mankind, because it's all me, me, me. What can I get out of it? How can I be better or live better than the other guy? I want power, riches, this and that. Satan makes things look so good, so beautiful. But it's all deception. And man buys into it. Hook, line, and sinker to use another of your cliches.

Satan is the great con man. He makes sin attractive and desirable, then when you're sucked into it, he's got you.

The Kingdom of God on the other hand, is life, freedom, forgiveness, love, joy, peace, hope. There is no condemnation in my Kingdom. Your sins are totally forgiven, totally erased, because I paid for them myself on the cross.

Unfortunately, not too many people accept my way, my Kingdom.

There are consequences to sin, and they're not pleasant. Sin has a way of catching up to you, of destroying relationships and trust, of taking away hope and happiness. There's a penalty for sin. It's called death, spiritual death.

I came to take away those consequences, to pay your penalty. I suffered death in your place. I suffered humiliation for you, I suffered pain for you, I suffered the taunts and the laughs of Satan because of my deep, abiding love for you.

Tell me again what sin is.

Remember when you asked me about what I taught? I said that the highest priority in your life is to love God with all of your heart, all of your soul, and all of your strength. You are to love God first, before anyone else, and you are to love Him with all that you have. When you don't, that is sin.

Then everyone has sinned!

That's right. All humans sin. Not one person has ever measured up to God's standards.

Give me some examples of sin.

Sin is injustice, cruelty, evil, insolence, arrogance, pride, selfishness, rebellion, knowing to do right but doing wrong. Sin is any action, any thought or word, that does not show my love. Sin can even be inaction. Not doing something you should do.

So sin means not living the way God wants me to live?

That's right. Why do you think people fight and argue with each other? Why do they take what belongs to someone else, not just material things but their identity, their honor, their dignity? Why do they use other people to satisfy their own desires? Why do they kill and maim? Of course, God doesn't want you to live that way.

I see tears in your eyes. Does it hurt so much?

I created man to love other people, to love all of my creation, and most of all to love me. I feel pain and hurt when men reject me, when they reject each other. Feeling pain isn't just a human emotion. I feel it, too.

Let me tell you why this all happens. It's because of Satan. Satan is pure evil. He absolutely hates God. And because God loves you, and wants you to love Him, Satan wants to destroy you any way he can. He tempts you to do what you shouldn't do, he plants his ideas in your mind to lead you away from God, away from me. And he is so subtle about it. He makes it seem so good. Satan tells you that you are better than other people. That you are too sophisticated, too intelligent to listen to God talk. That your primary goal in life is to find pleasure, to make money, to become powerful, that it's okay to do whatever you want as long as it "doesn't hurt other people." Of course, that's a lie, part of the big con game.

So Satan—

Satan puts it into the heart of man to want, to grab, and to take. That's how he operates. Because *he* wants, and *he* takes, and *he* grabs. He wants the soul of man. I do, too. But I don't operate his way. I want people to love me unconditionally. To love me and choose me and serve me because they want to, because it's the greatest desire of their heart. Satan wants people to lust after their own needs and desires. When people give in to that, they're giving in to him and letting him take control of their lives. When he's through he just casts them aside. I never cast anyone aside who calls on me.

Satan has many names—adversary, devil, the evil one, the archenemy, the accuser. He hates, he denounces, he condemns.

All in the guise of someone or something man sees as beautiful and desirable.

Maybe you don't hate or condemn, but you put guilt trips on people.

No, I don't. Guilt trips are from Satan. He likes nothing better than for you to wallow in your guilt. I am just the opposite. I give hope, freedom, forgiveness, a second chance (and a third and fourth and nine millionth chance), and joy and peace.

I won't control how a person responds to my love. I won't control how a person lives their life, or how they love or don't love, or how they distort love. I gave man the ability to think for himself and to do what he wants to do. It's called free will. I don't control that. Only you individually can control that.

With all that free will running around, I would imagine that not too many people are going to follow your way. We like our free will.

You're trying to be cute. Don't. This is serious.

You're right, though, that not too many people follow my way. The way to heaven is narrow and relatively few people take it. You are either for me or you are against me. Either accept me or reject me, but don't compromise. Don't play games. Don't modify the message. It's black or white, either-or.

When I return to earth to establish my Kingdom, all people everywhere will finally see the truth. They will finally see that I am the only way to the Father, that I am the only one who can make a person acceptable to God.   But then it will be too late. When that day comes, the door will be closed.

Once the door is closed, they won't get in. They will pound on the door to heaven and cry out, "Open the door for us!"

But I will answer, "I don't know you!"

They will plead, "You taught in our streets, we even dined with you."

But I will say, "I don't know who you are! Get away from me, you evil people!"

Then when you have been thrown outside, you will weep and grind your teeth because you will see people coming from all directions, sitting down to feast in God's Kingdom. The ones who are now least important will be the most important, and those who are now most important will be least important.

You don't want that to happen, do you?

No, I don't. But I have to let people exercise their free will. They can't be robots. That doesn't work in my Kingdom. Still I am concerned. I know what people are thinking, I know their motives. I can see their hang-ups, their hurts. I can see where they're phony and where they're sincere. I can see around the corners of their lives.

I'm concerned about things that come out of the heart. Not how you dress, not what you eat, not your social customs, but your inner being.

I designed you with a longing for God. You're not complete when that inner longing is unfulfilled. You can't live your life the right way when you try to fill that void with something other than God. In fact, you can mess yourself up pretty badly without Him. That longing, that void, can only be filled by Him. There is happiness no other way.

I was the perfect teacher, the perfect example, the perfect sacrifice. As a human, I was the only one who could satisfy God's high standards. I was a model to show you what you can become, how you can truly live, and how you can appropriate the power to live that way. My death put you right with God and gave you a fresh start. That's why I said I died on that cross to set you free, to liberate you from the bondage of sin, from those things that tie you into moral knots, to free you from the stranglehold Satan puts on you.

I died so that you will live. Not that you might live, not that you could live, but that you will live.

I urge you to give your life to me and see what I can do with it. The supreme argument for me is not intellectual debate, but to experience my changing power. That's the acid test.

You don't make it easy, do you?

It's not easy, but it is easy. The bottom line is, it's life changing.

I need time to think…

That's good. I want you to think about what I'm saying.

Who is responsible for my sin?

You are. Not God. Not Satan. You. Satan is the great tempter, the great con man. But you are responsible for giving in to that temptation, for buying into his program.

Why?

As I said, God has given every person a free will. You make your own choices, your own decisions. You are free to make good decisions and bad decisions. Free will makes evil possible, but it also makes the possibility of love, goodness, and joy worth having.

God has set before every human the choices of right and wrong, of life and death. He doesn't choose for you. You choose. And you reap the consequences.

So what's the bottom line?

First, I want you to realize that God loves you, more than any human could ever love you. The Father loves you, I love

102

you—just the way you are. I see through your outward wrappings, your bluster, your doubletalk, your macho image, your self pity. I see you as you are. And I love you.

Second, I want you to respond to that love, to love me in return, to believe who I am and what I did for you on the cross. I want you to commit your life to me.

I want you to ask me to forgive you of your sins. All of them. You don't have to name them, but you can if you want. You probably have forgotten most of your sins; some of them you will probably never forget. You might even have trouble forgiving yourself for some of the things you have done or thought. But if you ask me for forgiveness—and you mean it—I will forgive all of them. They will be gone, wiped out, obliterated. Sheer, instantaneous liberation. Freedom.

Do you know what will happen then?

No. But I think I want to find out.

You'll be a new and different person. You'll be transformed inside out. Your emotions, your mind, your very being will be transformed. You'll see life from a new perspective. So much so that you'll feel clean inside. There will be a fresh newness in all you do and think. I don't promise that everything will be sunshine and roses. Satan will still try to tempt you and lead you astray. People might ridicule you like they taunted me. But I will be with you—my Spirit will live in you—and I will help you over those bumps and through those valleys.

Is this what they call "born again?"

Yes. I know that people joke about this "born again" thing. But all jokes aside—all sarcasm and all preconceived ideas aside—this is truly being born all over again and starting out new. It's living the way God wants you to live.

What is hell like?

Let's talk about heaven. What is it like?

No, not yet. Let's talk about hell first.

Why all these negatives—sin, hell? I mean, I can understand somewhat about sin now. But hell?

Before you can know what heaven is like, you need to know what hell is like.

Okay. Tell me about hell.

Remember that I said God is Love?

Yes.

And that He is just and fair and good?

Yes.

That means He doesn't play favorites. He knows your heart, your motives, what you are really like. No one is perfect, everyone makes moral and ethical mistakes, everyone sins. God gives everyone the capacity to choose. You know—free will. While He loves everyone with a compassionate, all-encompassing love,

He allows you to choose either to follow Him or to reject Him. At the same time, He provides forgiveness, a "second chance," if you genuinely want forgiveness and a second chance. He doesn't play games, but He offers "second and third and fourth chances" as often as you want them, again, if you are genuine about it.

What the Father wants is for you to accept me, His Son, into your life. He wants you to believe in me, to put your trust in me. I am His son who died on that cross to take your punishment for your sins. Once you put your trust in me, you become His child, you become part of His family. If you reject me, and you die without me, you will spend eternity in hell, with no more second chances or forgiveness.

Now that's pretty straight forward, isn't it?

As you said earlier, there are consequences for what we believe or don't believe. Is that what you're talking about?

That's right. There are consequences. One of those consequences is hell.

But you have said repeatedly that God is love. How can a loving God send someone to hell?

God doesn't send anyone to hell. You send yourself to hell. It's your choice. Looking at it from a human perspective, if you don't involve God in your plans, if you don't involve Him in your life, why should He involve you in His plans and in His life? Now understand this—God hates hell, and he hates it when people choose to go there. God takes no pleasure in the eternal death of those who have rejected Him. He has reached out to you in many ways throughout your entire life. He has tried to break through to you, to get your attention. He has even provided a way for you to come to Him—through me.

Remember? I am the way, the truth, and the life. If you reject God and His way, and make the choice to go your own way and live the way you want, why should He pat you on the head and say, "Oh, I'm so sorry. Let Me take you in, even though you've been a bad little boy or girl? You've rejected Me? No problem. Let's just hold hands and skip off into paradise together." No, He doesn't operate that way. Love is tough. It involves forgiveness, yes. But it also involves justice and fair play.

To put it another way, God is a judge. The ultimate judge. He detests that which is not good. He detests injustice and unfairness and evil. He is outraged by the obvious stuff—murder, rape, embezzlement, child abuse, terrorism—but He is also offended by the "little" stuff—lies, jealousies, back biting, all the pains that humans inflict on other humans. In reality, there is no difference in God's justice between "major" and "minor" sins. Sin is sin. Period. Day after day, year after year, God lets these sinful actions go on. But there is coming a day when He will say "No More." He will let you spend eternity in the bed you've made for yourself…in hell.

I've got to go back to this love thing. If you love so much, why is there even such a thing as hell?

There's a hell because those who don't respond to me, those who don't love me in return, have no place in my heaven. They have their own place. Again, that's called hell.

I guess we'd better define hell. What is it? A burning lake of fire and brimstone? A place of total darkness? Gnashing of teeth?

Yes, yes, and yes.

How can it be all of those?

Hell is a place of torment where pain and suffering are unending, where there is eternal unhappiness. For some, hell is an eternal fire, for others it is eternal darkness, for still others it is a place of never ending remorse and anguish and despair. Hell is a cosmic garbage dump where all that is unfit for heaven will be thrown.

Hey, that scare tactic won't work for me. That's going too far. You almost had me convinced. That's not really the way it is. That stuff is just symbolism.

Are you sure? Then think about this. Hell is the total absence of God. Absolutely complete separation from God. It's the total absence of what is good, what is right, what is moral, what is beautiful.

And God sends people there.

You haven't listened, have you? God doesn't send anyone to hell. You send yourself to hell. Okay?

If you say so.

I do say so.

Damn, you make it hard.

No, you make it hard. Quit fighting. Listen to your heart.

Everything you've said is so compelling. I've never encountered anyone like you before. But I'm afraid. I want to believe. But...

You're comfortable, aren't you? You're afraid that involving me in your life might move you out of that comfort zone?

Yeah. That's what makes it so difficult.

I know. I understand. It's not something you want to take lightly. That's why I say, "Listen to your heart." Listen to the cry of your inner self. Listen to the very core of your being.

Okay. I...I will.

Let me say it again and again and again. My Father is the most generous, loving, wonderful, attractive being in the cosmos. He has made you with free will, and he has made you for a purpose, to love Him and to love others. You are not an accident, you are not a mistake. But if you continue to reject Him and His love, and to reject me, the Father will have absolutely no choice but to give you what you've asked for all along—separation from him.

Is hell a forever thing?

Yes. Just as heaven is forever, hell is forever. Let me say something that might surprise you. All humans live forever. When you die physically, your spirit continues to live on. Those who believe in me will live eternally with me in heaven. Those who don't believe in me will live eternally in hell.

That's not symbolism. It's the way it is.

What is heaven like?

Now can we talk about something much more pleasant? What is heaven like?

Heaven is incredibly alive. Everything, everyone, every activity, every moment in heaven is incredibly alive.

It's so alive you wouldn't understand if I tried to describe it to you. You wouldn't be able to comprehend how glorious it is, how awesome it is. Your language, your emotions, your experiences on earth are so inadequate.

Can you give us some idea, though?

The life you know here on earth is like being in a dark room, a totally pitch-black room. Even though you can't see anything, you get used to it, and you think it's the norm. Then someone suddenly lights a candle. Pow! That tiny little light explodes in your brain. It hurts. It's too much to behold because you're not used to it.

That's just a candle.

When I came into the world, I brought light because I am Light. My light blotted out the darkness. My light was not a mere candle, but a spotlight, a forest fire, as bright as the sun.

Imagine that heaven is much more brilliant than that. So much brighter, so much more vivid, so much more intense. God's holiness absolutely permeates heaven with a perpetual brilliance of light and colors. It's a light that doesn't hurt, but that envelops you, comforts you, frees you. Your sense of touch, your sense of smell, everything is so heightened, so intense, so real, there's substance to it. You'll see things in a way that has not been possible for you before. If you've been sighted, you'll see the total spectrum of light and non-light. If you've been blind, you'll see…well…it'll "blow your mind," to use one of your clichés. And the colors—ah, you can't envision the intensity of the colors, the variations of shades, colors you've never seen on earth. Light and colors that are alive, pulsating with energy.

This will sound foolish, but what does heaven sound like?

More beautiful than anything you've ever heard on earth. All of creation sings—the stars, the galaxies, clouds of cosmic dust swirling in and through the universe, soaring and melodious, like a swelling symphony orchestra with a life of its own, every instrument playing its own song, but all of it harmonious and complementary, tunes weaving in and out of all the other tunes into a beautiful fabric of joy and praise.

In heaven trees, grass, flowers, rocks, mountains, rivers, meadows, forests all undulate to the music of angels and believers alike—rolling and billowing to the rhythm of the music, worshiping, spontaneous, free, liberated.

What will we look like?

"We?"

You've really had me thinking...

It's difficult for me to say this...but...I believe. I believe. I really believe.

No more playing games...no more trying to be what I'm not, no more trying to be my own god...I ask your forgiveness, I put my trust in you. I want your Spirit to live in me. And I want you to forgive my sins, all of them...Clean me out, make me new, be my God.

Welcome home! Do you hear that music, those cheers? All of the angelic beings in heaven, all the saints, all those who inhabit the heavenly places, the Father, Himself—all of heaven is resounding with praise at your confession. It's joyously deafening, isn't it?

Heaven is your home, and I'm looking forward to your coming home. You'll be with me for eternity.

What will you look like in heaven? You'll look like you do now, and you'll be absolutely beautiful, inside and out. You'll be in the presence of Almighty God, and His glory will be reflected on you. You'll look the way I originally intended for you to look when I created you. You'll look like yourself, and you'll look like me, all wrapped up in one fantastic package.

In heaven will I recognize people who are there? I mean, will I recognize people in the Bible, people in history, people today who are believers? Or will I have to be introduced to them?

Oh, you'll know them. You'll know exactly who's who. And they'll know who you are, too. There'll be no introductions. You'll know each other. Even those you don't know, here on earth, you will know there. Oh, and that baby that was miscarried,

113

or that was aborted, or that died maybe a year or two or three later—you'll know that baby. And that baby will know you. It'll be a grand reunion.

Can I ask you a question that is kind of off the wall? I've heard people say that when humans get to heaven, they become angels. Is that true?

I imagine that Gabriel is chuckling to himself right now. No. Humans don't become angels. They don't earn wings. They don't sit on clouds strumming harps. Neither do angels, for that matter. There really are angels, but they're an entirely separate creation from humans. Angels are God's messengers. They exist to do His will. There are times when angels interact with humans on earth because the Father has sent them to do that. Sometimes on earth angels look like humans and sometimes like the spirits that they are. You'll get to know angels in heaven, just like they know you here on earth.

What is there to do in heaven? I mean, I'm new at this, and I've got a lot to learn, but walking for eternity on golden streets, and sitting beside a crystal river, and singing all day just seems kind of boring.

Believe me, heaven is not boring. Heaven gets deeper and fuller the longer you are there. Heaven is an everlasting adventure with God. The Father has an assignment for each person in heaven. Assignments are meaningful and challenging, based on each individual's talents, abilities, and spiritual gifts. You won't do exactly what you do on earth, but what you do will be extremely satisfying, extremely gratifying. If you like to serve, you'll serve. If you like to study and learn and investigate, you'll be studying and learning about the totality of God's creation. If you like to sing, you'll be singing and praising. Whatever gives you the most pleasure and satisfies you the most on earth, will be multiplied many times over in heaven. Oh, no, there's no such thing as "boring" in heaven.

Heaven is the land of the redeemed, of the free. Heaven is filled with absolute happiness, absolute joy, absolute peace. Physical infirmities, mental illness, emotional hang-ups, tears, hurts, misunderstandings do not exist in this glorious place.

Do you like to dance?

Well, yeah, I guess so. But I'm not very good at it.

In heaven you're going to dance. You're going to dance with me. People in wheelchairs will dance with me. Quadriplegics will dance with me. People with ALS and muscular dystrophy and cerebral palsy and Parkinson's and Alzheimers and with amputated legs and the blind and deaf and addicts and the depressed and the abused and the homeless and the poor and the rich will dance with me. Farmers and shop keepers and politicians and lawyers and doctors and teachers and mechanics and plumbers and soldiers and truckers and housewives and the young and the old will dance with me.

That's what heaven is like.

When are you coming back?

Teach me, Lord, to dance! I'm ready!

That's what I want. I want you to always be ready.

When are you coming back to take us home?

I don't know. Only the Father knows. And He hasn't told me yet.

It is close, though, isn't it?

I think it's very close. But don't go up on a mountain top and wait for my coming. That won't speed it up. I want you to go about the tasks I have given you to do. Feed the hungry, house the homeless, care for the less fortunate, proclaim the good news about me around the world. Don't focus on my return, but focus on me.

I don't want you to be caught up in endless speculation about the end times. Every generation since I left the earth 2,000 years ago thinks the time is at hand. But you must be patient, you must strengthen your resolve, you must be ready because my coming is drawing near.

When people say to you, "Look there" or "Look here," don't go looking for me. When I return, it will be like lightening flashing across the sky. You don't know when it's going to happen, but when it does, it will happen so suddenly you won't have time to get ready for it.

I'm going to return only for those who are ready, for those who believe in me, who have committed their lives to me, who call me "Lord" and "Savior."

What will it be like? Two people will be sleeping in the same bed, but only one will be taken. The other will be left. Three people will be in the same room, but only one will be taken. The other two will be left. Many will be in school or at work or in the fields, but only a few will be taken. The others will be left.

Again I say, be ready. Prepare for my coming. Devote yourself to doing my work. Read my Word. Pray.

Why is prayer important?

You emphasize prayer a lot, so it must be important. But what exactly is prayer? Why should I pray? Where should I pray? When should I pray? Do you always answer prayer?

Whoa! There you go again, all kinds of questions. But that's okay. I like questions. They give me a wonderful opportunity to teach.

Now that you are a believer, let me teach you three things—how to pray and worship, how to live the Christian life, and how to get ready for my return.

First, let's talk about prayer. Yes, it's very important.

Prayer is, quite simply, talking with me. Prayer is sharing your innermost feelings with me, your hopes, your dreams, your fears, your frustrations. I want you to talk with me. Out loud or quietly or in whispers or in silence. It doesn't matter. I hear you when your prayers are still in your heart, even before you voice them.

119

When you pray, don't be pious, don't put on, don't try to impress me. Don't say the same words over and over until they don't mean anything. I want you to talk with me from your heart, your soul. Talk to me about everything. I want to hear it all. Don't make prayer an escape strategy, a last-minute, last-ditch thing. I mean, that's okay. I hear those prayers, too. But I want you to make prayer an essential part of your life. That's what I want.

Yes! That's what I want, too.

You see, prayer is being in touch with the eternal, everlasting, almighty, holy, awesome God. He has invited you, through me, to be His partner in working out His will in your life and in the lives of others. Isn't that amazing? Humbling? God wants you to partner with Him in the working of His will in people's lives. Prayer is a God-given opportunity to shape the eternal lives of His people.

The Father wants you to delight in Him. If you do, if He is truly the delight of your life, He will give you the desires of your heart. Prayer is not getting God to do what you want. It's not manipulating Him. It's about your getting on the same page with Him and wanting what He wants, desiring the same things He desires.

What does He want?

He wants you to walk intimately with Him. He wants you toabide in Him.

How do I do that?

That's up to you.

When you find what it means to walk intimately with someone, to abide in them, and to let them abide in you, then you will know what it means to abide in Him.

120

Can you imagine how responsive your heavenly Father is to you because you are His child? You see, the most important thing to God in all the cosmos right now is what's happening in your life. Your life occupies His attention. You matter to Him more than you can possibly know. God is deeply interested in your prayers because He is supremely interested in you. You have His heart and you have His ear. So pray.

Pray about the big stuff and pray about the little stuff. It doesn't matter when, it doesn't matter where, just pray. God is listening. He never sleeps, He never slumbers. Be bold. Count on the fact that He hears you and that He responds to you. God is not bothered by your coming to Him in prayer. He's not inconvenienced by your request. He's not reluctant to give you all that you need. He will never turn a deaf ear to one of His beloved children.

Who should I pray to?

You can pray to the Father, or to me, or to the Holy Spirit. It doesn't matter. We are one. There's no "magic" formula.

What should I pray about?

Whatever you want to pray about. Remember, prayer is conversation between you and me. As I said, I want you to share your heart, your feelings, your dreams, and your hurts with me.

Prayer can involve praise. It can be thanksgiving. It can be asking for forgiveness and giving forgiveness. It can be asking for help and asking how you can help. Prayer can be intercession, praying for someone else. Prayer can involve meditation on the greatness and power and might of God.

How long should my prayers be?

It doesn't matter. You can speak to me in words or sentences or paragraphs or entire pages, even entire chapters. Let it flow.

Once in a while stop and listen for my response. Just be quiet and listen. You might not hear me if you're not very good at listening. But keep listening. You'll hear me.

When should I pray?

Whenever you want to. When you wake up, when you go to bed, in the middle of the night, while you are working or playing or driving or talking to someone or quiet or noisy.

Forgive me for being naive, but do I have to close my eyes when I pray?

Don't worry about being naive. No question is naive. Close your eyes? If you want to. Some people find that closing their eyes helps them focus on what they are saying without getting distracted. But that's up to you. I don't care if you pray with your eyes open or closed.

Going back to when I should pray…

I want you to pray all the time. Non-stop. A word here, a word there, kind of a stream of consciousness.

You prayed, didn't you?

I prayed every chance I got, which sometimes wasn't often enough. One day, for example, I was told that my cousin, John the Baptist, had been beheaded. I immediately wanted to go off by myself and pray to my Father about it. Just to talk with Him, to unload my sorrow on Him.

But people crowded around me all morning long to be healed. I looked forward to healing them, to see their bodies and minds whole and refreshed.

And then that afternoon and into the evening, the crowds got hungry as they listened to my teaching, 5000 men plus women and children. So I took time to feed them. Just a few loaves of bread and some fish, but oh how it refreshed them.

Finally, late in the day, I had a chance to get away and pray. What a glorious time to be alone with my Father, to pour out my soul to Him. When I came down from the mountain, my disciples were in trouble on the Sea of Galilee. It was storming, and they were afraid their boat would capsize. I walked to them—on the water—and stilled the storm. I reassured them that I was in control, even of the weather. They were safe in my hands. What a day! Just about every day was like that. I rarely had time to myself, so I got up early and stayed up late so I could pray. Prayer to me was not a requirement, it was a privilege. A breath of fresh air in my life.

Did you say that meditation a kind of prayer?

I did. When you meditate, you deliberately think about something for a long time. You kind of roll it around in your mind, you "chew on it." It's like a cow chewing on her cud, again and again, getting all the good she can out of it. Or a dog chewing on a bone to get all the tasty marrow.

You can meditate on the holiness, the awesomeness of God. His incomprehensible ways. His infinite wisdom. His glorious promises. You can contemplate God's divine majesty or power or kindness or redeeming love.

Meditation is kind of like a music of the soul, where you get lost in it and feel its rhythms envelope you and become one with you.

Would you like me to teach you how to meditate?

Sure. I want to learn all I can. I'm not used to meditating. I've never really done it. In a busy world like ours, how can you get off by yourself and just think? I mean, that's hard to do, and I don't think—

Be still.

I don't know if I can be still. My mind just keeps going and going, you know, and I'm always thinking about this problem I have at work, or relationships with others. There's always something going through my mind, how am I supposed to keep still? How am I supposed—

Be quiet.

...to keep quiet? There's always noise. The TV, the radio, cars honking, neighbors yelling, dogs barking. You go to the mall, and it's so noisy; you go to a game, and it's really noisy, especially if your team is ahead; you get in the car, and even the tires make noise. You get home, and the phone rings. Well, actually, my phone rings all the time wherever I am. Even in the bathroom. I don't really think—

Are you through yet?

I can't do this meditation stuff. There's no time for it. Oh, I wish I could take time. It sounds like something I should try. But even then, I don't think I'd have time to do it. This meditation stuff seems kind of deep. Do you think I could get to know you better that way? After all, I do want more of you in my life, or is it you want more of me in your life? I don't know—

Shut up.

I'm sorry. I just kept on talking and talking. I have a lot to learn, don't I?

Yes. But you'll get there.

Meditation is just keeping still, isn't it?

Yes. "Be still, and know that I am God." That's a good verse for you to memorize. Sometimes believers can be so busy, even in doing my work, that they have no time for me. I want you

124

to take time to listen to me. I want you to be still, block out the noise, and listen, because in those moments you will know that I am God.

I have more questions about prayer. Do you always answer prayer? Are there some prayers you answer, some you don't, and some you say wait a while?

I always answer the prayers of believers. Sometimes you don't hear my answer, or don't recognize my answer, or don't want to accept my answer. Sometimes I say yes. Sometimes I say no. Sometimes I say wait.

Your prayers are in my hands. Not in your hands, but in my hands. I want you to talk to me, to let me know your needs, your desires, and your wants. Then leave it to me. Don't try to outguess me, to "out answer" me. I know that most of the time when you ask for something, you go through all the possible answers in your mind. Let me tell you something. I often answer in ways you never thought of, and they're better answers than you could ever think of, perfectly tailored to your ultimate good and happiness, and to the Father's ultimate glory.

Sometimes I allow pain into your life. It hurts, and you wonder, "Where's God? Why has He abandoned me?" The truth is, I have not abandoned you. You had to experience the pain to get to the better answer. For example, surgery hurts. There is sometimes intense pain. But the doctor is not trying to hurt you. He's trying to heal you. The end result is better health, or better mobility, or longer life. But you had to go through the pain to get there.

So sometimes you say yes, even though I may have to experience pain first. Why would you say no to my requests?

When you pray for selfish reasons. When you ask for the wrong thing. When you ask for the right thing but with the wrong motive. When what you pray for is not in accordance with the will of God.

Let me give you an example. Paul prayed that God would remove the thorn in his flesh. He felt that it was a hindrance to his ministry. He prayed a lot about it because it bothered him so much. But what he didn't realize is that God wanted him to have that problem. It was a reminder to Paul that he was always to keep his mind on me. His ministry was too important in establishing the early church for Paul to have his mind wandering all over the place. He had to stay focused. The "thorn in his flesh" helped him to stay focused, helped to keep him humble, so that he would find his strength in me. He was such an obstinate man, such an intellectual man, and, yes, such a proud man, that without that thorn he would have been tempted to put his faith more in himself than in me. As it was, his strength was in me because of the "thorn."

I'm not as strong as Paul was. I have trouble with "no" answers. But I guess I have to accept them. They're for my best good, aren't they?

Yes.

What about "not now, but later" answers?

Sometimes you ask for the right things at the wrong time. You don't have the perspective that God has. In time you will get what you are asking for, but right now you couldn't handle it. It wouldn't be good for you.

If the answer to your prayers doesn't come when you think it should, wait for it. It might seem to take a long time. But don't worry. My timing is always perfect.

126

How often should I pray about something? I mean, should I pray just once, or should I keep on praying and praying and praying?

There's another verse in the Bible that I want you to memorize. It's in Revelation at the very end of the New Testament. "Ask and you will receive. Search and you will find. Knock and the door will be opened for you." What it means is that you are to continually ask me, and you will receive. Continually search and you will find. Continually knock and the door will be opened.

Let me tell you a story about how you should keep on praying and never give up. There was once a crooked judge who didn't believe in fairness. He believed in under-the-table judgement. In that same town there was a poor widow who had been wronged by someone. She went to the crooked judge and said, "Make sure that I get fair treatment in court." She kept on asking, day after day after day. The judge refused to do anything. No money, no favorable judgement. But the widow wouldn't give up. Finally, in exasperation the judge said to himself, "I really don't care about this widow, but I'll grant her request because she keeps on bothering me. If I don't help her, she'll wear me out."

Even more so, don't you think a just and fair God will grant the requests of His children who pray to Him day and night? Won't He be concerned for them?

Another story. A neighbor's friend arrived from a long journey and was hungry. The neighbor didn't have food because he wasn't expecting the friend so soon. So the neighbor went next door to ask for food. But it was midnight. The owner of the house was in bed and didn't want to be bothered. Yet because of the neighbor's boldness and persistence, he got out of his comfortable, warm bed and gave him as much as he wanted.

In the same way, God takes care of His children when they come to Him with boldness and persistence.

So God wants me to come to Him boldly and to be persistent in my asking?

That's right.

Does it really matter if my prayers are answered or not?

Then why pray if it doesn't matter? Of course it matters. As I said, your prayers are always answered, although maybe not always the way you would like them to be answered.

Let me ask a similar question. If God already has the answers worked out, then again, why pray? The answers are preordained.

No, they are not preordained. God has a plan for your life. But He works out His will through the prayers of His children. Your prayers make a difference because they demonstrate where your heart is, the sacrifices you are willing to make, and your commitment and resolve. God wants you to partner with Him in the outworking of His will on earth. You have been given the awesome privilege of joining God through prayer to see His will done.

Does God just snap His fingers and my prayers are answered?

No. God started answering most of your prayers long before you were born. Indeed, the foundation for some of your prayers was laid when the universe began. To answer even one prayer—whether it's a yes, no, or wait answer—involves working in the lives of many people, many of whom you have never met.

The seed of that answer involves a circumstance here, which impacts on an event there, which further impacts on a person there, and so on, like a long chain, all intricately linked together, long before the answer gets to you. And that's just one prayer!

I never realized it was so complicated.

It's not complicated to God.

So prayer really does change things?

It sounds so trite to say that prayer changes things. But it does, primarily because prayer changes you. You make yourself vulnerable when you pray, and that gives me the opportunity to bring that change about.

What are my prayers like to God?

Your prayers are like incense to the Father. A sweet smell. There are God's servants in heaven (they are called the 24 elders) who fall on their face before the Lamb (that's me) to worship me, holding in their hands golden bowls filled with incense, the prayers of God's people. To put it in today's vernacular, your prayers smell awfully good to God!

I want you to imagine the adventure of prayer. I want you to imagine what will happen when you pray earnestly for God's will to be done in your life and in the lives of others. I want you to imagine knowing without a doubt that God hears you, and you will get what you've asked for because you've prayed according to His will. I want you to imagine that your prayer is His prayer, that your heart is His heart, that you are on the same page with Almighty God.

Prayer can be that real and that powerful if you seek God's will, if you obey Him in everything, if you share everything with Him—with me. No imagination involved. You can do it.

Why is worship important?

What is worship?

From the very beginning, man has worshipped whatever he wanted to—animals, trees, the stars, the moon, the sun, mythical creatures, a multitude of "gods." Even today you worship your gods—movie stars, heroes, philosophies, ideologies, technology, dictators, "spiritual" people, money, prestige, accomplishments. The list is endless.

But—I want you to understand this—you are *not* to worship any of these *things*. You are not to worship created things, but to worship only the One who created them.

Do you understand? You are to worship the Creator and not the creation. There's a tremendous difference. You are not—you are absolutely *not*—to worship or pray to or bow down to anything that has been created. That includes things and people here on earth, and things and created beings in the heavenlies.

I know I'm going on and on about this, but it's so important. You are not to worship angels, demons, or Satan. You are to worship only the Creator—Almighty God. He alone is Lord. He alone is holy, infinite, all powerful. He alone is worthy of your adoration, your praise, your worship.

So what is worship? It is reverence, a sense of awe, an awareness of my presence. Worship is joy, trust, loyalty, love, gratitude, dependence, obedience, service, thanksgiving, praise, meditation.

Worship can be individual. Just you, alone at home, in the countryside, on the lake, in the mountains, in the desert, even in the middle of a crowd of people where you can shut them out and just be alone with me.

Worship can be corporate, where you join with others in a sanctuary, tabernacle, temple, synagogue, upper room, outdoors.

Worship can be quiet, internal, in your thoughts. Worship can be out loud, using your voice or a musical instrument, or an exclamation of emotion. Whatever your mode of worship, you are to worship in a sense of spirit and truth.

What does that mean?

To worship me in spirit means that your worship must spring from your heart. It must be sincere, it must be honest. Worship is more than just words. It is an offering, a giving of your life to me, your affections, your appetites, your desires.

To worship me in truth means to acknowledge me as ultimate Truth, ultimate Wisdom, ultimate Intelligence, ultimate Love. To use one of today's words, your worship must be transparent. You must come to the throne of God without pretending to be something or someone that you are not.

This is all so new to me. What does it mean to praise you?

Praise is joyful worship, acknowledging who I am and what I do—my majesty, my holiness, my works of creation, my redemptive acts.

Where worship can be quiet or out loud, praise is most often out loud, an outward emotion, an outpouring of gladness and rejoicing. Praise can be an exclamation, a testimony to others about my working in your life. You can praise in song or prayer, individually or collectively, spontaneously or prearranged. Praise can spring from your emotions or from your mind.

Like prayer, praise should be continual. Praise should always be on your lips.

You want me to smell good?

You said you wanted to teach me three things—one was prayer, the second was how to live…

Remember when I said that your prayers are like incense to God? A sweet smell?

Yes.

In the same way, I want you to smell good to God.

You want me to "smell" good?

I know, it sounds funny. But I'm serious. You know how important smell is in your everyday life, don't you? Smell influences how food tastes, how you react to other people.

I know what you're talking about. Decaying garbage smells absolutely horrible. For that matter, so do bad breath and body odor and a lot of other things I could mention. But the smell of a hamburger on the grill, ah, that smells good. And the smell of someone I love, as subtle as that might be, really attracts me to that person.

I never thought about it before, but smell is a pretty powerful influence, isn't it?

Smell is a powerful influence here and in the spiritual world. Evil and sin smell putrid. On the other hand, forgiveness, kindness, and love have a sweet, delightful smell. Those who believe in me smell absolutely wonderful.

Do I do smell good to you?

Yes, indeed. And I want you to keep on smelling good.

How do I do that?

By staying close to me, standing side-by-side with me every moment of every day. By living a life that is loving, patient, peaceful, gentle, faithful, in control of your thoughts and your emotions.

The one thing I don't want you to do is to give in to sin, as tempting as it may be at times. What seems enjoyable at first can lead you into all kinds of problems.

Before I met you I did a lot of things that I thought were enjoyable, like drinking with my buddies. I enjoyed sex, I liked partying—

Did you? You didn't like the hangovers. You didn't like the drunken arguments. The sex wasn't that fulfilling. Sometimes you looked awfully foolish at those parties and wished later you hadn't said or done some of those things. You might have told yourself that this stuff was "fun," but later it wasn't, even when you and your "buddies" embellished your accomplishments and bragged about them.

How do you know all this?

I was there.

Even then, when I had no idea who you were?

I knew all about you, but I left you alone to do your thing. Those were your choices, and I don't interfere. But still I loved you and prayed to my Father for you.

You amaze me more and more. I mean, you're the God of the universe. You've got all this big stuff to be concerned about. And yet you were concerned about me. Unbelievable!

That's the kind of God I am.

Am I going to have fun in my new life in you?

How do you feel now?

Pretty darn good. Clean. Free. Alive.

Are you having fun?

I don't know if "fun" is the word for it. I'm not the same person I was before. Things are different somehow.

But you know, I am having fun. Talking with you. Man! You're challenging. Emotionally, intellectually, every which way. It's a different kind of fun, and I like it.

I know. God's parties are so much more satisfying than Satan's parties, aren't they?

Yeah, so much more fulfilling. And no hangovers!

Okay, let's go on to the next step in your learning to live your new life. Let's talk about temptation.

Yeah, we talked earlier about whether you were ever tempted. I was kind of sarcastic. I apologize.

Apology accepted. I was tempted, yes, in every way that you'll ever be tempted. Now that you've put your faith in me, Satan is going to fight hard to get you back. He doesn't like losing. He's going to lay temptations on you to get you away from me, to make you doubt, to lead you back to the life you had before.

I can handle that.

Not by yourself, you can't.

Here are three rules that will guide you when you are tempted.

One, you've got to involve me when you are tempted. Don't ever leave me out. I've been there, and I know how to help you.

Two, you must understand that temptation, itself, is not sin. Giving in to temptation is sin. Satan knows what your weaknesses are, and he'll exploit them. He knows what might work and what might not work.

Are you saying that if my weaknesses are not like smoking or drinking or gambling or power or money, then Satan most likely will not tempt me in those areas? But if my weakness is sex, or whatever, he'll probably exploit that all he can?

Exactly. Since he knows your weaknesses, you've got to know what those weaknesses are and avoid them. Don't give Satan any opportunity to tempt you.

Is it possible to stop these temptations before they even begin?

YES. Most emphatically yes. Don't wait for them to get full blown; stop them at the beginning. Most temptations begin in your mind, in your thoughts. Don't give in to those thoughts. Flee from them. They are like a roaring lion intent on devouring you. Don't even give them a chance. That's why I said to involve me from the very beginning. Let me be your strength, your defender.

Now, Satan is sneaky. Because you're a believer, he'll often use Scripture to justify the temptation. But he'll twist it to his own means. He tried those tactics on me. You should counter his attacks the same way I did, by looking him straight in the eye and telling him *no*. Then use Scripture, yourself, to refute his arguments. Scripture is God's Word. It's powerful because the Holy Spirit indwells the very words of Scripture.

Rule Number Three. Never forget that Satan has absolutely no authority over you. Do you understand that? Let me say it slowly. Absolutely...no...authority. I have forgiven your sins, I have taken away any claims he might have over you, I have set you free from him. I have authority over your life now. He doesn't have any authority over you. He no longer owns you. I do. Do you understand?

For once I do.

Now, let's talk about obedience. To obey me is one of the most important aspects of your new life. When I want you to do something, do it. Don't question it, don't try to get out of it. Do it.

How do I know what you want?

First, read the Bible. As you do, the Holy Spirit will speak to you. Sometimes words and verses will just leap out at you. At other times, you'll discover my will for you more deliberately as you study and absorb my Word. I want you to read the Scriptures with a prayerful attitude, with an open mind and an open heart, with a sense of expectancy.

How will I know that the Spirit is speaking to me?

The Holy Spirit will speak to you in different ways. It might be a simple feeling or thought. It might be a gnawing in your mind or heart that grows and grows until you can't escape it any more. It might be an "aha" moment.

I don't have a problem with that. In fact, I think I'll enjoy reading your Word.

That's good. I want you to read my Word as often as you can. Get to know it. Hide it in your heart so it's there when you need it.

The Holy Spirit might speak to you in other ways, as well. He might speak to you through other people, through a book or a newspaper story, through an incident or situation in your life, maybe even through a dream or a vision. The Holy Spirit communicates in many ways. The main thing is to listen to what He is saying to you, then do it.

I want your Spirit to speak to me, like you're speaking to me now. But in all honesty, I think I'll have problems with that "don't question it" part. I have to know what I'm getting into before I commit myself. I have trouble with blind trust.

Let me tell you about Moses.

Was he the burning bush guy?

Yes, he was the "burning bush guy," and the guy who parted the Red Sea so the people of Israel could escape from Egypt, and the guy I gave the Ten Commandments to.

Moses was a born leader with a great compassion for my people, the Israelites. But when I told him to go to Pharaoh—the king of Egypt, the most powerful man in the world at that time—and demand that he let my people go, Moses argued with me. He didn't argue just once but again and again. His problem was that he didn't think he was good enough.

Moses had a string of arguments. "Who am I?"…"I'm nobody."…"Who will I say sent me?"…"If I say God sent me, they won't believe me."…"What if they think I'm crazy and making all this up?" Moses wasn't through. "I'm really not a good speaker. I'm slow, and I can never think of what to say." Finally, "Hey, Lord, please send someone else to do it."

The arguments didn't work. Moses did what I wanted and became a great leader of his people. But he lost a tremendous blessing by not being able to speak my words directly to the king and to my people. I appointed his brother Aaron to speak for him, to be his mouthpiece.

What I'm saying here is that I want you to trust me. I'm not saying to throw your intellect out the window, I'm not advocating that you rush into something blindly.

That's good because I have a brain, an intellect. You gave it to me when you created me. I like to think things through rationally and logically before I commit myself.

I know. And I'm saying that's all right. I want you to be yourself, to use the abilities, the talents, the mental processes I gave you. What I'm saying is trust me.

However, when I tell you explicitly to do something, I want you to do it. At that point, don't argue or say you need more time or even that you need to think it through. That's where the "blind" trust comes in. I'm telling you to obey me because it's important and I know what's best for you.

It's not that easy, you know.

I know it's not easy. But remember that obedience is part of my love for you. Just as I was obedient to the Father by going to that cross and suffering all that pain and death, so I want you to be obedient to me. I want you to demonstrate your love for me by obeying me.

Okay? Let's talk about the next step in learning how to live your new life. Remember when you asked if I ever got angry? If I ever laughed? If I ever cried?

Yes.

I want you to learn to get angry, I want you to learn to laugh, I want you to learn to cry.

What do you mean?

I want you to get angry about injustice, about man's inhumanity to man. Don't just sit back and let it go by. Do something about it. Getting angry isn't just words. It's actions, too. It's doing something about the wrong choices people make, about ungodly attitudes. If you have to throw the money changers' tables over, do it. If you have to stand for righteousness, do it.

At the same time, I want you to learn to laugh, to enjoy yourself, to rejoice in the wonderment of life, in the value of other people. I want you to let loose, to celebrate me, to celebrate each other. Live life to the fullest. I created life to be enjoyed. So...enjoy it. Be genuine. Be real. Be my people in this hurting world.

And I want you to learn to cry. You don't have to preach at people, to always give "solutions," or to say "I told you so." Learn to put your arm around people and cry with them.

I want you to learn to love—

I'm sorry about my being so sarcastic when you talked about love earlier. I didn't know what true love was. I do now. Help me to learn. Teach me. What does it mean to love God with my whole heart? With my whole being? With my whole understanding? With my whole strength?

It's a radical love. It's the love that sent me to the cross. Are you sure you want to know more about it? To love that way yourself?

Yes.

It's the love I want you to have toward me and your fellow man. And toward yourself. An unselfish love. A forgiving love. A no-strings-attached love. Can you do that?

Not on my own! That's a pretty amazing love. I need you to help me. I don't know how to love "everyone." How do I love someone I don't know? Like a dictator, or a Prime Minister, or a Queen, or a President? Or someone in a foreign country? Or the owner of my company, or—

Or the family on the other side of town?

Yes.

I know them. Ask me to take care of them, to be with them in their needs, to comfort them, to show my love to them. You might become part of my plan. I might ask you to get acquainted with them and to help them in tangible ways. If I ask you, then do it.

How do I love someone I do know?

Be there for them. Don't intrude, but be there. Listen, cry, laugh with them. Help as you can—food, clothing, shelter, money. Don't expect anything in return.

What does it mean to love someone who's suffering, in pain?

Be there. Listen. Embrace them. Try to feel their pain. Don't offer solutions. Just be there. You are to be like the good Samaritan. Help those who need help, take care of them, bind up their wounds. Do not pass by on the other side.

What about my own suffering? When I have health problems, or financial problems, or marital problems. What am I supposed to do? How do I handle it? I mean, this is pretty serious stuff.

143

I've been there. I know what it's like to suffer, to be despised, to be broken. I was betrayed, sold out. I loved, and I was rejected.

Put yourself, your circumstances, your life in my hands. I won't despise you or betray you or reject you.

It seems so simplistic.

What I'm saying is not simplistic. In fact, if you are really listening to me, what I am saying is profound.

Let me tell you something. Those who have suffered the most are often those who have the deepest faith. They've been there, gone through it, and have come out of it with a faith that can conquer anything. Not because of what they've done, but because they learned to rely on me.

In every department of your life—your work, your family life, your finances, even your spiritual life—you will have your ups and downs. There are times when things will be great. Couldn't be better! Then there will be times when you feel numb, powerless, discouraged. Nothing goes right.

What about—

I'm not finished. I wish you didn't have these ups and downs. I wish you were always "up." It's so difficult to walk in the valleys. It can really hurt. Even those around you, the ones you love the most, can be affected by your pain. There's no easy answer. But the bottom line is, come to me. I'm here. I can heal you, I can ease the pain, I can bring you through.

You see, my desire is that you rely more and more on me. I don't promise to take away the hurts. But I do promise that I will go through those hurts with you. I promise that I will strengthen you, that I will make you more into what I want you to be, that I will help you grow from a milk-fed babe into a mature believer.

When all else fails, call on you?

That's okay, but how about involving me from the very beginning, then all else won't fail.

What does it mean to love someone who hates me?

Just that. Love those who don't love you. Do good to those who hate you. Bless those who curse you. Pray for those who abuse you. And do this all the time, not just once in a while when you feel generous.

To the person who strikes you on the cheek, you must also offer the other cheek. I mean that. Literally. To the one who takes your things, you must not demand them back. I mean that, too. This is tough love, isn't it? Tough on you. And life changing to the one being loved.

There are some people who say they have sinned too much, they have done despicable things, or led horrible lives, and don't deserve forgiveness. What do you say to them?

I can forgive anyone, no matter how awful they think they have been. My heart's desire is to forgive them. But forgiveness must start with them. They must want to be forgiven. They must ask me for forgiveness, and their request must be sincere. I don't hate them. I love them. I love them so much that I gave my life for them.

What about people who say they love you, that they have committed themselves to you, that they pray and believe your promises and try to do good. But they don't see you working in their life. They ask "Why?" "Where are you, God?" "Why aren't you helping me?"

I will tell them most emphatically "Trust me. I'm here. Let me do what is best for you. Let me do it on my timetable. I won't let you down."

145

What about people who say they are good people? They have lived good, moral lives. They have never hurt anybody, never cheated anybody. They have always done what they could to help other people.

No one is perfect. All have sinned and come short of God's expectations. Only one man has ever been perfect, and that was me. Everyone needs God's forgiveness. Everyone needs to believe, to commit their life to me. I don't want you just to know *about* me. I want you to *know* me.

What does it mean to be a "good" Christian?

I don't know. Either you're a believer or you're not a believer. There's no in-between.

So, we've talked about "smelling good," obedience, learning to laugh and cry and get angry, and love. You said this new transformed life wouldn't be difficult. It sure seems difficult to me.

My way is easy. Your way might be difficult. You have to forget about "me, me, me," and start depending on "Me." Do you understand the difference? It's not you, but me. I am just as real today as I was 2,000 years ago when I walked this earth. I am just as concerned about you today as I was about all the people I touched back then. I want you to put your absolute trust in me. Involve me in all your decisions, large and small. Involve me first, let me lead the way.

If you do that, what an exciting life you'll live!

In a sense, living your life in me is unbelievable. But it's real! And doable!

You want me to wear the Emperor's clothes?

Okay, you've talked about prayer and how to live the way you want me to live.

Number three, I want to teach you how to get ready for my return. Do you understand that?

Yes.

Are you with me?

Yes.

Okay. Now listen carefully. You're a believer. You've put your faith in me, you've turned away from your sins and asked for my forgiveness, which I've gladly done. You're dead to yourself with all your lusts and desires, and alive with a new life in me. Your thoughts have been cleaned up, and my thoughts and attitudes have become your thoughts and attitudes. In short, you have been born again.

Are you still with me?

Yes.

Over the centuries my followers have always faced difficult times. Even now around the world there are countries where believers face starvation, persecution, torture, and death. As my return gets closer, more and more of my people will suffer persecution and death. You, yourself, might face persecution.

Why?

Because the people of this world hate me, they will hate you, too. The more you stand up for me, the more they will hate you. Satan knows these are the last days, and he's going to pull all the tricks out of his bag to turn people against me. He doesn't want people to believe in me. He wants them to believe in him, as perverse and misguided as that may be.

When the people of this world hate you, remember that they hated me first. When they persecute you, it's because they persecuted me first. People will do to you exactly what they did to me.

You're scaring me.

No, don't be scared. I'm telling you these things to keep you from being afraid. I will always be with you. You will never be alone.

Even so, I want you to be wise and on your guard. The time will come when your children, your parents, your friends might turn against you. You might not be allowed to meet with other believers. You might not be allowed to even say My name in public. The time will come when many believers—perhaps even you—will be arrested and taken to court. You will be beaten and tortured. You will stand before judges, governors, or military tribunals and given a chance to deny your faith. If you deny me, they will set you free. If you hold fast to me, you will suffer the consequences.

Now listen carefully.

148

The consequnces might include death. People will think they are doing God a favor by killing you. They will do these things because they don't know me. All they will know will be the lies of the devil. Satan is very good at deceiving people, and most of the people in this world will be deceived by him and will actually declare him to be god.

When these things happen, do not worry about what you will say or how you will defend yourself. You will be given the right words when the time comes. You will not be the one speaking. My Spirit will be speaking through you.

A long time ago some of my followers faced these same things. At first they were weak and trembling with fear. They were scared, terrified. But they decided to forget about themselves and how they might defend themselves, and to simply let God's Spirit show His power through them. When the authorities beat them and warned them not to speak about Me, they kept on speaking about Me anyway. They considered it worthy to have been persecuted on behalf of My name. Day and night they continued to teach and proclaim the good news from house to house. Regardless of the outcome. And the outcome for most of them was death.

Did they willingly die? They must have really been committed to you. You died for them, and they died for you. I wish I could have met some of them.

Yes, they willingly died. They knew the Truth, and they were willing to die for it. I want you to be like them.

And, yes, you will get to talk to them someday, all of them, and many more besides who have died for me over the ages, and many more who didn't get the chance to die for me, but lived just as passionately for me.

I'm telling you all this now so that when the time comes, you will remember what I have said. I have prayed to my Father to keep you safe through the power of My name. Even in the midst of persecution, torture, and death I will give you peace. It's the kind of peace that only I can give. It isn't like the peace that this world can give, so don't be worried or afraid. I want you to be faithful to me until the end.

You don't allow cowards into your Kingdom, do you?

My Kingdom is literally a matter of life and death. I can't have soft followers. I must have courageous followers. Either you are for me or you are against me. If you deny me, I will deny you before my Father in heaven. If you acknowledge me, I will acknowledge you before my Father in heaven.

Where do I get that courage?

Your courage comes from me. I am your resource, your well, your filling station. When you are low on courage, come to me for filling, and My Spirit will fill you again and again and again to overflowing.

So I need to be courageous, to come to you when I need more courage, more strength. What else must I do to get ready?

I want you to wear the Emperor's clothes.

I don't understand.

I want you to wear the clothes I will give you.

I already have a closet full of clothes. I don't need any more.

Yes, you do. The clothes I give you are spiritual clothes that will allow you to stand against the wiles of the devil and to keep on standing. It's not a one-time thing, this warfare we're in. It's a continuous warfare that won't end until I throw Satan and his minions into the fires of hell, banished from my presence forever.

Because your enemy is spiritual, it takes spiritual clothes and spiritual weapons to fight the good fight of faith.

What are these clothes?

A belt, a vest, a coat, shoes, and a hat. I want you to also carry a sword.

A sword? That's old-fashioned, isn't it?

We're talking about serious things. So don't make light of it. I'm giving you what you need to be victorious in your spiritual battles. When I say there are clothes I want you to wear, I mean it. When I say I want you to carry a sword, I mean it. These are not games we're playing here. Are you with me?

Yes.

Here's what I want you to wear every day in order to fight effectively against the forces of Satan.

First, I want you to wear a belt around your waist. It's a belt of truth. My truth. I have already set you free from every guilt, fear, and depression that the enemy may launch against you. But he's going to keep hammering away at you with guilt, fear, and depression. He's going to try to wear you down. As long as that belt of truth is cinched tight, it will strengthen and protect your innermost being against Satan's lies.

Next, I want you to put on a strong, tough, impenetrable vest that will stop even a frontal attack by Satan. It's a vest of integrity, purity, and holiness. This vest will protect your heart from lust, perversion, and deception——the lies and temptations that Satan will continually throw at you.

151

The shoes I give you will allow you to walk in the peace of God. Though the way through life is rocky sometimes and overgrown with thistles and has numerous switchbacks, you can walk with confidence wearing my shoes. They will keep you from danger and allow you to walk in purpose and determination regardless of the difficulties and dangers thrown up by Satan.

Over your belt and your vest, and reaching down to your shoes, I want you to wear a coat of faith that will be your first line of defense against the fiery darts of the wicked one. As long as you are wrapped in faith, you are secure and safe. This coat provides 360 degree protection, keeping you from being caught off guard by Satan's attacks.

I want you to wear a hat that will protect your head from the blows of the enemy. You see, your head is the dwelling place of your mind and soul. The greatest battlefield is in your mind. This is the area that the enemy wants to attack the most, because the mind is where deception takes place, where doubts begin, where wrong desires germinate, where error takes root. The hat that covers your head represents your salvation, and reassures you that you belong to me, and I belong to you. It is my covering over you.

You must always carry with you a double-edged sword. The sword is my Word hidden in your heart. It is only through the Word that you can meet Satan head on and go one-on-one with him. You cannot hope for victory in this spiritual battle without your sword, sharpened and ready to repel Satan's attacks.

Every day as you put on these garments and the sword, I want you say, "Lord, live this day through me. Protect me. Keep me from harm. I put my faith and trust in you."

No one can take away my love for you. I love you today, I will love you tomorrow, and I will love you forever. I will never leave you nor forsake you. You belong to me. I died for you. I conquered death for you.

This sounds like a farewell.

I am leaving, but only for awhile. I'm going to prepare a place for you where you will live with me forever. When the time is right, I will be back to gather you to myself.

Your Majesty!

Oh, Lord, I bow down to you and declare your glory, your majesty!

The time is coming when the entire creation—all that has been and all that is and all that is to come—will bow before Me and declare My majestsy.

My Father ordained from the very beginning that I would leave the glorious riches of heaven and represent Him on earth. When My time on earth was finished, and I had accomplished all that the He had wanted Me to do, He placed Me at His own right hand in the heavenly places, far above all spiritual powers and dominions.

My Father exalted me to the highest place in the spiritual world and gave me a Name that is above every name, and that every knee should bow, in heaven and on earth and under the earth, and every tongue confess that I am Lord, to the glory of God the Father.

What is that Name that is above every name?

Wonderful Counselor

Prince of Peace

Prince of Life

Alpha and Omega

the Beginning and the End

the Bright and Morning Star

Author and Finisher of Our Faith

the Resurrection and the Life

Christ

Messiah

Immanuel

Savior

Holy One

Horn of Salvation

Lion of the Tribe of Judah

Lamb of God

the Good Shepherd

the Chief Shepherd

the Gate

the Door

the Word

Word of Life

Word of God

Our Advocate

Light of the World

the Way

the Truth

the Life

Faithful and True

King of Kings

Lord of Lords

King of Righteousness

Son of God

Mighty God

Lord God Almighty

Lord of All

I Am

Jesus

You're not finished with me, are you?

This chapter is for you, the reader, to write, because it's about you.

If you desire to accept Jesus into your life, to become one of His followers, say the following prayer in all sincerity and truthfulness. Change the words to fit your situation, to express how you feel, if you wish.

> Dear Jesus. I want to know you as my Savior. I want you to clean me out, to make me a new person, to fill me with your love and your Spirit. I am sorry for my sins, for rejecting you, for trying to live my life on my own without you. Please forgive me. Please come into my life. I believe in you and give myself to you. In your name I pray. Amen.

That's it. God has been knocking on the door of your life for as long as you have been alive. Maybe you've heard the knocking, maybe you haven't. But if you said that prayer, and you meant it, you have opened the door and let Jesus into your life. You have a new identity and you belong to a new family. You have a new Father who will never let you down!

Learn about this new relationship. Immerse yourself in it. Read the Bible, perhaps beginning with the Gospel of John. Read the Psalms, the song book of the Bible. Read Proverbs, great guidelines for living each day.

Read other books that talk about the faith—personal stories of other believers, commentaries about the various books in the Bible, deeper studies about Bible subjects. Learn from others who have been there and studied and learned and discovered.

Pray as often as you can, sharing your life and your aspirations and your feelings, yes, and even your doubts, with your Lord.

Find a good church to attend—a church that teaches the Bible and bases its authority on the Bible. Get involved in that church, in the Sunday morning services, the Sunday evening services, the Saturday services, the Friday services, whenever they are. If they have small group meetings in members' homes, get involved in one of those, or in the youth meetings or the men's or women's or couples or seniors meetings. If you are addicted, or are a single parent, or divorced or widowed, and they have those types of meetings, get involved in those.

If you have a talent for singing or playing an instrument or acting or lighting or audio or TV or stagecraft, get involved. If your heart aches for people who are sick or in prison or are homeless or shut-in, get involved. If your talent is finance, business, advocacy, or writing or teaching, get involved.

I know, that's a lot of "involves." But involvement is the key to becoming what God wants you to be.

Get to know your fellow believers. Study the Bible with them. Pray with them and for them. Build your relationships with those who were in your life before you made this commitment to Jesus—your mother or father, your spouse or best friend, your co-workers, fellow students, teachers. Tell them about your new life, how Jesus has changed you and how He can change them.

In the midst of this, find a mentor, a person you can feel comfortable with, a person who's been a believer for a while. Your mentor should be someone you can open up to, someone you can confide in, someone you can have lunch with to talk things over, someone you can call at midnight to pray with, to laugh with, to cry with. Someone who can help you grow in the faith.

Get ready. *Jesus is coming back.* And you will dance with him in heaven for eternity.

19
Now what?

Much of this interview is based on Scripture, specifically the Gospels of Matthew, Mark, Luke, and John. Matthew and John were eye witnesses of the life of Jesus since they were among the Twelve disciples, the ones closest to him during his three-year ministry. Mark was a companion of the apostle Peter. Though Mark was not an eye witness, he wrote what Peter told him about Jesus, and Peter, of course, was an eye witness, one of the Twelve. Luke was a traveling companion of the apostle Paul, a Pharisee who became a follower of Christ after His crucifixion and resurrection. Paul is responsible for the major spread of Christianity throughout the Roman world. Luke, a physician and historian, wrote his biography of Jesus based on eye witnesses he interviewed, people who had been close followers and others who had heard the stories from eye witnesses.

Some of this interview with Jesus is speculation. We don't know, for example, that Jesus worked as a carpenter in

Sepphoris, a city that isn't even mentioned in the four Gospels. But we know from history and archaeology that Sepphoris was a thriving Jewish-Roman city in the time of Jesus. It was a cultural center and the administrative center of the Galilee region of north Israel until Herod moved the administration to the city of Tiberias on the shores of Lake Galilee. We know, also, that Sepphoris was just five miles from Nazareth where Jesus grew up, an easy walk in that day and age. So it's a good guess that Jesus walked to Sepphoris many times and he was familiar with the city. It's also a good guess that Jesus and his earthly father, Joseph, sought work as carpenters there.

Other speculation—we know that Jesus was angry at times and cried at times. We don't know that he ever laughed. The Gospels don't mention any incidences of laughing. But he was a joyous person who enjoyed a good party and loved children, so it's safe to say that he laughed and probably enjoyed a good joke. The Gospels say nothing about his everyday habits, but again, it's a good guess that he brushed his teeth, however they brushed their teeth in that time, that his clothes got dirty and had to be washed, and that he had "bad hair days."

If you want to read the stories and descriptions yourself in the Gospels, here are some scriptures that can be a starting point. There are more scriptures that aren't listed here, so search them out and read them as you are led. Many Bibles have footnotes or concordances that list references to certain words and verses.

By the way, there are many translations and paraphrases of the New Testament and the entire Bible. Read the one you feel most comfortable with.

Let's explore, chapter by chapter:

Chapter 1. You were a radical, weren't you?

For a description of how the people of Nazareth reacted to Jesus, read Luke 4:16–30.

About Jesus being homeless, read Matthew 8:20.

Jesus attracted huge crowds who wanted to hear and be healed by him. See Matthew 4:23–25.

Nicodemus, one of the religious leaders, met clandestinely with Jesus at midnight. That conversation is recorded in John 3:1–21.

Among those who called Jesus "God" were Peter and Martha. See Matthew 16:16 and John 11:27.

Jesus affirmed that He was the Son of God in Mark 14:61–62. See also John 10:31–33.

For Jesus healing lepers and interacting with them, read the story of the ten lepers in Luke 17:12–19. Only one of the ten came back to thank Jesus.

Tombs or caskets in those days were often above ground and were covered with whitewash. Matthew 23:27.

The religious leaders said John was possessed by a demon. Read Mark 1:4–6, then Matthew 11:18.

To get the full picture of what the leaders thought about Jesus, read Matthew 11:19, then John 8:48 and John 10:19–20.

167

The story of the adulterous woman is found in John 8:1-11.

Jesus didn't take political sides. See Matthew 22:15-22.

Read the story of the Roman centurion in Matthew 8:5-13.

Chapter 2. Why did you heal?

The story of the woman with the bleeding problem is told in Luke 8:43-48.

The story of Lazarus being raised from the dead is found in John 11:1-44.

The synagogue ruler's daughter is brought back to life by Jesus in Mark 5:21-43.

Peter and John heal the man crippled from birth. Acts 3:1-10.

Some blame a man's crippled condition on sin in John 9:1-5.

Jesus healed very few people in Nazareth because of the town's lack of faith in Him. Read Matthew 13:54-58.

Chapter 3. What did you teach?

Jesus' justification for His ministry, his healings, and his teachings, was in Isaiah 61:1-2 and Isaiah 42:7. He read those scriptures in religious services at Nazareth in Luke 4:16-21.

Jesus' primary message was that God loved the world so very much that He gave His only Son, that whoever believes in Him will not die spiritually, but will have eternal life. John 3:16.

Jesus spoke with authority, Matthew 7:28-29, and with power, Luke 4:36-37.

He preached that man's first duty is to love God. Matthew 22:36-38.

God takes care of those who love Him. Matthew 6:25-34.

Man's second duty is to love his neighbor as he loves himself. Matthew 22:39-40.

Loving yourself is not necessarily a thing of pride. Matthew 23:12.

Much of what Jesus preached about relationships, ethics, and love is contained in His "Sermon on the Mount," condensed into three chapters in Matthew, chapters 5, 6, and 7.

Chapter 4. Your mother was a virgin?

An angel appeared to Mary in Luke 1:26-38 and to Joseph in Matthew 1:18-25.

Mary visited her cousin, Elizabeth, in Luke 1:39-45.

The birth story telling about the shepherds in the field and the baby born in a manger is found in Luke 2:1-21.

169

A second place to read about Jesus' birth tells about the wise men from the East. It is found in Matthew 1:18-2:12.

The story about Joseph, Mary, and the baby fleeing to Egypt is in Matthew 1:12-23.

When Jesus was 12, he accompanied his family to Jerusalem where he spent three days in the temple with the religious scholars of his day. Luke 2:41-52.

Jesus performed his first miracle at a wedding, where he turned water into wine. John 2:1-11.

Religious leaders turned Jesus' family against him in Mark 3:20-35.

The prophet Isaiah predicted the coming of the Messiah (Jesus) and his virgin birth 700 years before it happened. See Isaiah 7:14 and the entire 53rd chapter.

Chapter 5. Did you ever get angry?

Jesus was angry about the buying and selling in the temple. John 2:13-16.

He was angry at the religious leaders who objected to his healing on the Sabbath. See Matthew 12:9-13.

He was angry at the lack of faith concerning the epileptic boy. Luke 9:37-43.

Jesus enjoyed parties and telling about happy endings that involved a party, such as the story of the prodigal son. Luke 15:11-32.

Jesus enjoyed playing with little children. Though the text doesn't say this outright, it is easy to see that Jesus would be laughing and playing with the children in Matthew 19:13-15.

The Scriptures say that Jesus wept when Mary took him to the grave of her brother, Lazarus (John 11:32-35), and when he felt sorrow over Jerusalem (Luke 19:41-44). The text doesn't say that he cried, but he probably did when Judas left the Last Supper to betray him (John 13:21-30), during his agony in the Garden of Gethsemane before he was arrested (Luke 22:39-46), and when Peter denied him three times (Luke 22:54-62).

Chapter 6. Tell us about your disciples.

About Jesus being tempted, read Luke 4:1-13.

Jesus tells about the prostitute who became one of his followers in Luke 7:36-50.

Another of his female followers, Joanna, is mentioned in Luke 8:1-3.

The brash Peter is described in Matthew 14:22-31, where he leaps out of the boat and walks on water toward Jesus; in John 13:2-9, where Peter has problems with Jesus washing his feet; and in Luke 22:31-34, where Jesus predicts Peter's denial.

171

Judas is sent out with the Twelve to preach and heal in Luke 9: 1-6, and his concern with money is told in John 12:1-6.

Jesus states the qualifications for being his disciple in Luke 14:25-27.

Chapter 7. How did you die?

What we call "Palm Sunday," when Jesus rode into Jerusalem on a donkey to signal the beginning of His last week on earth, is described in John 12:9-19.

The religious leaders decided to kill Jesus at a meeting described in Matthew 26:3-5 and John 11:45-53.

The religious leaders tell the people in Jerusalem to be on the lookout for Jesus. John 11:57.

Jesus predicts his death in Mark 10:32-34.

Judas betrayed Jesus in Luke 22:1-6.

Jesus' experience in the Garden of Gethsemane is found in Luke 22:39-65.

Jesus' flogging is mentioned in John 19:1-3 and the mocking of the soldiers is described in Mark 15:15-20.

Pilate released the murderer, Barabbas, in Luke 23:18-25.

Roman soldiers conscripted Simon to carry the cross in Mark 15:21.

Soldiers gambled for Jesus' clothing in John 19:23-24.

They used their spear shafts to break the legs of the two criminals crucified with Jesus, and one of them thrust his spear into Jesus' side in John 19:31-37.

Chapter 8. You didn't stay dead, did you?

The story of the resurrection of Jesus is told in the final chapters of each of the four Gospels.

Jesus' appearances following his resurrection are described in each of the four Gospels. Paul describes the post-resurrection appearances in some of his letters, for example in 1 Corinthians 15:3-8.

Chapter 9. Why did you go through all this?

The Bible doesn't try to prove the existence of God. It simply affirms that He is and that He is the one and only God. All other "gods" are false. Psalm 115:1-8.

Though the Bible does not specifically declare the Trinity, that one God functions as three separate, distinct persons, it does allude to this concept in a number of passages, such as Ephesians 2:18, Ephesians 3:14-17, and 2 Corinthians 13:13.

God is Spirit. John 4:24. He has no body as a human has a body. Thus, to us He is invisible. 1 Timothy 1:17.

As Spirit, God is incomprehensible to us. Job 36:26, Romans 11:33-34. Yet He is a person and makes Himself known to us. Ezekiel 38:23, Isaiah 66:13, Romans 1:19-20.

God is far above the human realm. Isaiah 46:5.

Yet He created man in His image, Genesis 1:26-27, as well as creating all that has been and ever will be created. Genesis Chapter 1.

The classic verse in the New Testament that describes why Jesus came into the world is John 3:16.

One of the early statements about the divinity of Jesus—the Word—and the declaration that He is creator is found at the beginning of John's gospel in John 1:1-3.

Jesus states that he and the Father are one in John 10:22-30.

An early hymn of the church about God breaking into history through His Son is found in Philippians 2:5-11. Another passage that affirms this is Colossians 1:15-20.

Jesus declares that he is the way and the truth and the life in John 14:6.

What is sin? See Jeremiah 2:5, Romans 8:5-8, and Ephesians 2:1-3.

All of mankind falls short of God's standards. Romans 3:23.

Jesus refers to both the kingdom of Satan and the Kingdom of God in Matthew 12:25-28.

Satan is called many things in Scripture—Ruler of this World, Prince of this World, the Devil, Tempter, Prince of Demons, the Accuser, and others. See John 8:42-44, 1 John 3:7-10 (this is not the Gospel but one of John's letters), and Ephesians 6:12.

Satan has so blinded this world that many people who think they are doing God's work will be left out of His Kingdom. Luke 13:22-30.

Sin emanates from the heart. Matthew 15:19.

God's tremendous love for mankind allows men freedom of choice, to accept or reject the gift of His Son. John 3:17-21.

Paul talks about reconciliation in Colossians 1:15-20 and 2 Corinthians 5:16-21. Peter talks about our being healed by His wounds in 1 Peter 2:24.

Read John 3:1-16 to find out what it truly means to be "born again."

Chapter 10. What is hell like?

God sent His Son into the world not to condemn but to save us. By inference, then, we send ourselves to hell. See John 3:17.

Yet there will come a time of judgement. See John 12:44-48 and John 5:24-30.

The Bible gives us several pictures of what hell must be like. One of those is the story of the rich man and the beggar in Luke 16:19-31. Another passage describing hell is Revelation 20:10.

Chapter 11. What is heaven like?

About Jesus being the Light of the world, read John 1:4-9.

The Bible gives us brief glimpses of heaven. The most descriptive passage is probably Revelation 21:1-22:5. Another, but shorter passage, is John 14:2-3.

Heavenly beings do, indeed, rejoice when a person gives their life to Jesus. Read Luke 15:8-10.

Will we look like Jesus in heaven? Maybe. See 1 John 3:2.

Are we going to dance in heaven? Probably. When the prophet Jeremiah describes the return of the children of Israel to their homeland, he is in a sense describing our homecoming to heaven, a homecoming that includes joyous dancing. Jeremiah 31:1-14.

Chapter 12. When are you coming back?

Although Jesus is returning to earth to take those who believe in Him to heaven, even He doesn't know when that will be. Only the Father knows. The entire third chapter of Mark talks about this, but you might particularly read Mark 13:32-37.

Chapter 13. Why is prayer important?

Though prayer is important, God doesn't care for pious, showy prayers. Matthew 6:5, 7.

Prayer is the sharing of your heart with God. Psalms 142:2, Psalms 62:8, Lamentations 2:19.

What does it mean to walk intimately with God? Read Galatians 5:16 and 2 Corinthians 5:7.

Jesus prayed in the morning (Mark 1:35) and at night (Luke 6:12). He prayed when He had a chance to get away from the crowds. Read the entire chapter of Matthew 14.

The Bible talks about meditation in Psalms 119:97, Joshua 1:8, and Philippians 4:8.

You can read about Paul's "thorn in the flesh" in 2 Corinthians 12:7-10.

The story of the widow and the judge is in Luke 18:2-8.

The story of the neighbor's friend who came at midnight is in Luke 11:5-8.

Your prayers are like incense to God. See Revelation 5:8.

Chapter 14. Why is worship important?

A most wonderful passage describing worship is 1 Chronicles 29:10-13.

Another is the entire 100th Psalm.

In the New Testament, heavenly worship is described in Revelation 4:8-11 and 5:11-14.

Worshiping God in Spirit and in Truth is found in John 4:23-24.

Chapter 15. You want me to smell good?

Believers really do smell good to God! Read 2 Corinthians 2:14-16.

Read about Jesus' Temptation, and how Satan uses Scripture, in Matthew 4:1-11 and Luke 4:1-12.

Another passage that talks about Jesus being tempted is Hebrews 4:14-16.

I Corinthians 10:13 describes how we can overcome temptation.

Hide the Scripture in your heart. Read Psalms 119:11.

The Holy Spirit speaks to us through Scripture. See 2 Tim 3:15-16, 2 Peter 1:20-21, Acts 17:11.

It's very important that you obey God. Read Leviticus 18:4-5 and John 14:1 and 14:21.

Don't argue with God as Moses did in Exodus 3:1-4:17.

Use your intellect to explore, investigate, and ascertain all of God's creation, but still obey Him. Romans 12:2.

Learn to love. Read John 13:34-35 and John 21:15-17.

Love those you don't know. Read Romans 13:8-9.

Love those who are suffering, those who are hurting. See 1 John 3:16-18.

Love those who hate you. Matthew 5:43-48 and Luke 6:27-31.

When you feel that you are having a valley experience, that things aren't going well, read the 23rd Psalm as well as Philippians 4:10-13. Another Scripture that might apply is 2 Timothy 4:5.

Jesus says that His way is easy. See Matthew 11:28-30.

Chapter 16. You want me to wear the Emperor's clothes?

Jesus talks about the end times in Matthew 24:1-44.

The Holy Spirit took control of the situation when Peter and John were brought before the authorities. Acts 4:1-31.

Paul spent quite a bit of time in prison, such as described in Acts 16:22-40.

When you are put on trial for your faith, the Holy Spirit will speak through you. Luke 12:11-12.

Paul describes the armor of God in Ephesians 6:11-18.

Then He says "Be of good cheer. I have overcome." John 16:33.

Chapter 17. Your Majesty!

The day will come when every knee will bow before Jesus. Philippians 2:5-11.

Jesus is called "Wonderful Counselor," "Prince of Peace," and "Mighty God" in Isaiah 9:6.

He is "Prince of Life" (or "Author of Life") in Acts 3:15.

He is "Alpha and Omega," "the beginning and the end" in Revelation 1:8.

Jesus is "the bright and morning star" in Revelation 22:16.

He is "the author and finisher of our faith" in Hebrews 12:2.

He is "the resurrection and the life" in John 11:25.

Jesus is called "Christ" in Matthew 1:16 and "Messiah" in Daniel 9:25.

180

His name is "Immanuel" in Isaiah 7:14.

He is "Savior" in Isaiah 19:20.

He is called "the Holy One" in Mark 1:24.

He is "Horn of Salvation" in Luke 1:69.

He is "Lion of the Tribe of Judah" in Revelation 5:5.

John the Baptist describes Him as the "Lamb of God" in John 1:29.

Jesus calls Himself "the Good Shepherd" in John 10:11.

Peter calls Him "the Chief Shepherd" in 1 Peter 5:4.

Some Bible translations call Jesus "the Gate" and some call Him "the Door" in John 10:9.

Jesus is "the Word" in John 1:1, "Word of Life" in 1 John 1:1, and "Word of God" in Revelation 19:13.

He is "Our Advocate" in 1 John 2:1 and "Light of the World" in John 8:12.

Jesus is "the Way, the Truth, and the Life" in John 14:6.

Riding on a white horse, He is called "Faithful and True" in Revelation. 19:11.

He is "King of Kings" and "Lord of Lords" in Revelation 19:16.

He is "King of Righteousness" in Hebrews 7:2.

He is "Son of God" in Luke 1:35.

He is "Lord God Almighty" in Revelation 4:8.

He is "Lord of All" in Acts 10:36.

He is "I AM" in Exodus 3:14.

And He is to be called "Jesus" in Matthew 1:21.

George Pettingell has interviewed hundreds of people on radio and television for over 20 years. He created and co-hosted the daily *Focus* interview show on the national Family Radio Network based in San Francisco, and is producer and host of the weekly *Public Report* interview program on Trinity Broadcasting Network's Seattle station, KTBW-TV.

He has directed public relations activities at hospitals in Louisiana and Texas, and was Public Information Officer for the U.S. Peace Corps' Dallas office.

George lives in Federal Way, Washington, with his wife, Karen. They have three children and six grandchildren.

If you would like to order additional copies of
Teach Me, Lord, to Dance: An Interview with Jesus
please see our web site at
www.frankiedovepublishing.com
or write us at
Frankie Dove Publishing
P.O. Box 3875
Federal Way, WA 98063

CPSIA information can be obtained
at www.ICGtesting.com
Printed in the USA
JSHW020239051019
1822JS00001B/3